THE MIGHTY THOR

AN ORIGIN STORY

Based on the Marvel comic book series **Thor**
Adapted by **Rich Thomas**
Interior Illustrated by **The Storybook Art Group**

MARVEL

New York

visit us at www.abdopublishing.com

Reinforced library bound edition published in 2013 by Spotlight, a division of the ABDO Group, PO Box 398166, Minneapolis, MN 55439. Spotlight produces high-quality reinforced library bound editions for schools and libraries. Published by agreement with Marvel Press, an imprint of Disney Book Group, LLC.

Printed in the United States of America, North Mankato, Minnesota.
042012
092012
♻ This book contains at least 10% recycled materials.

TM & © 2012 Marvel & Subs.

Library of Congress Cataloging-in-Publication Data

This book was previously cataloged with the following information:
Thomas, Richard.
The mighty thor origin storybook / By Richard Thomas ; [edited by] Michael Siglain.
p. cm.
1. Thor (Norse deity)—Juvenile fiction. 2. Superheroes—Juvenile fiction. 3. Humility—Juvenile fiction. I. Title.
PZ7.T36933 2012
[E]-dc223

2010938698

ISBN 978-1-61479-011-2 (reinforced library edition)

All Spotlight books are reinforced library binding
and manufactured in the United States of America.

marvelkids.com

What would it be like to *live among* **legends**?
To be something **more** than human?

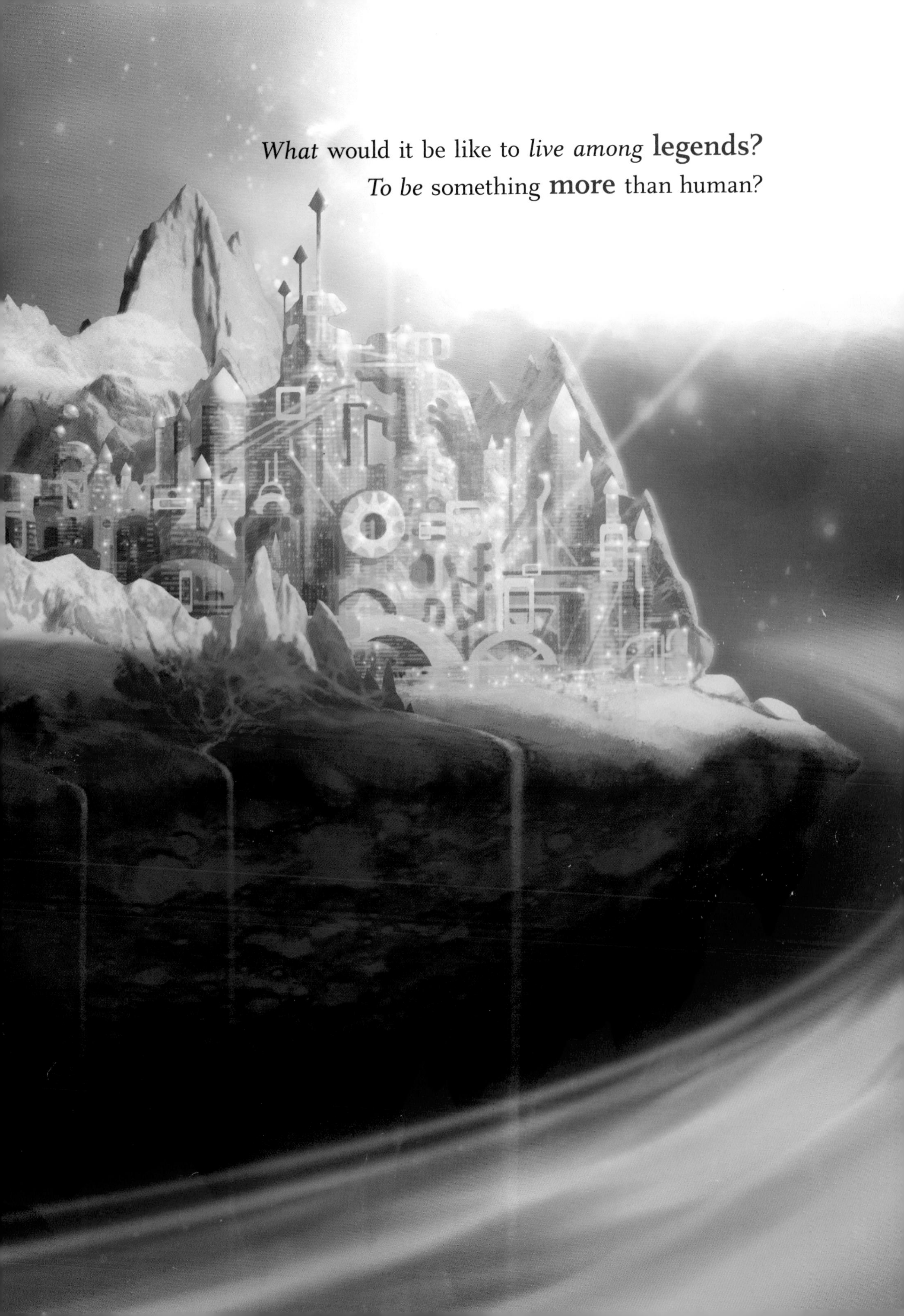

To hold **great power** in your hands

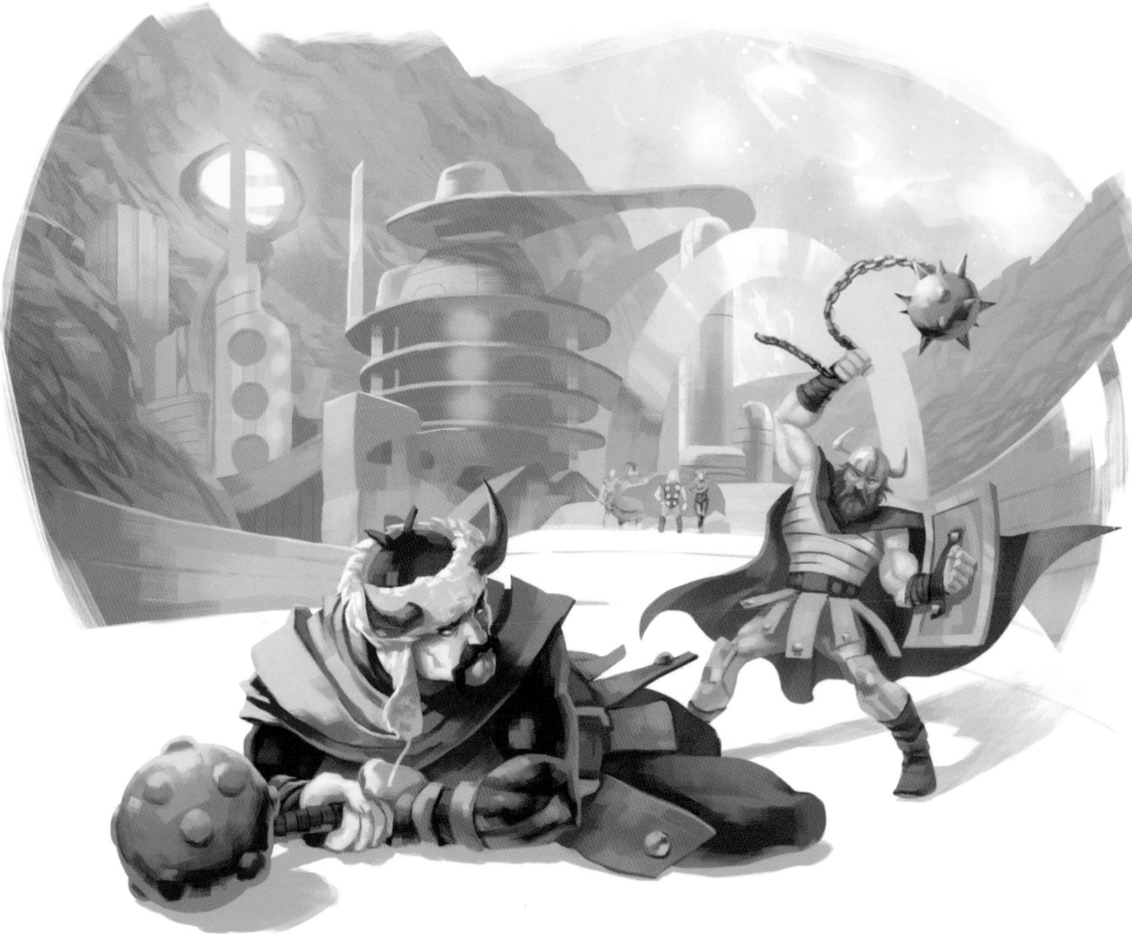

and know how to **use** it?

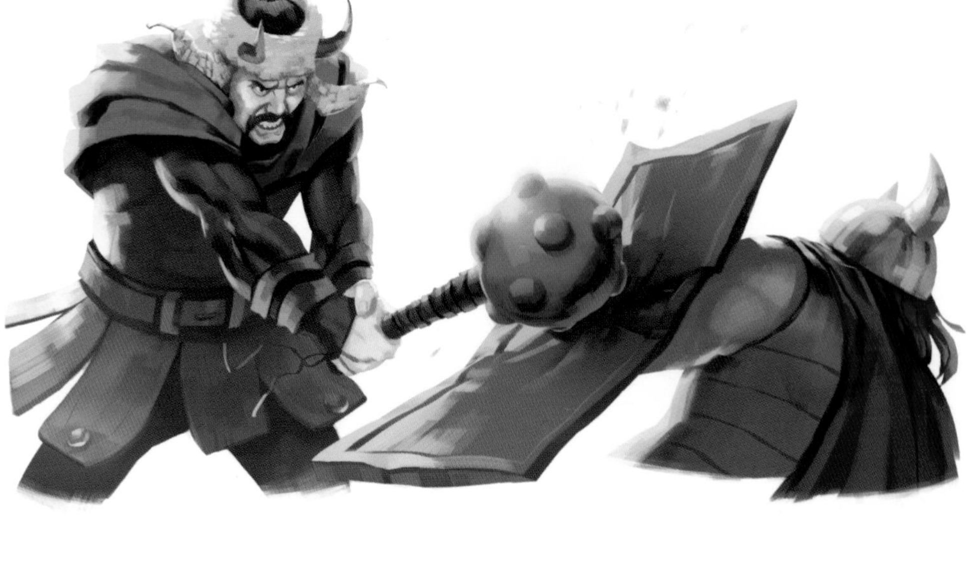

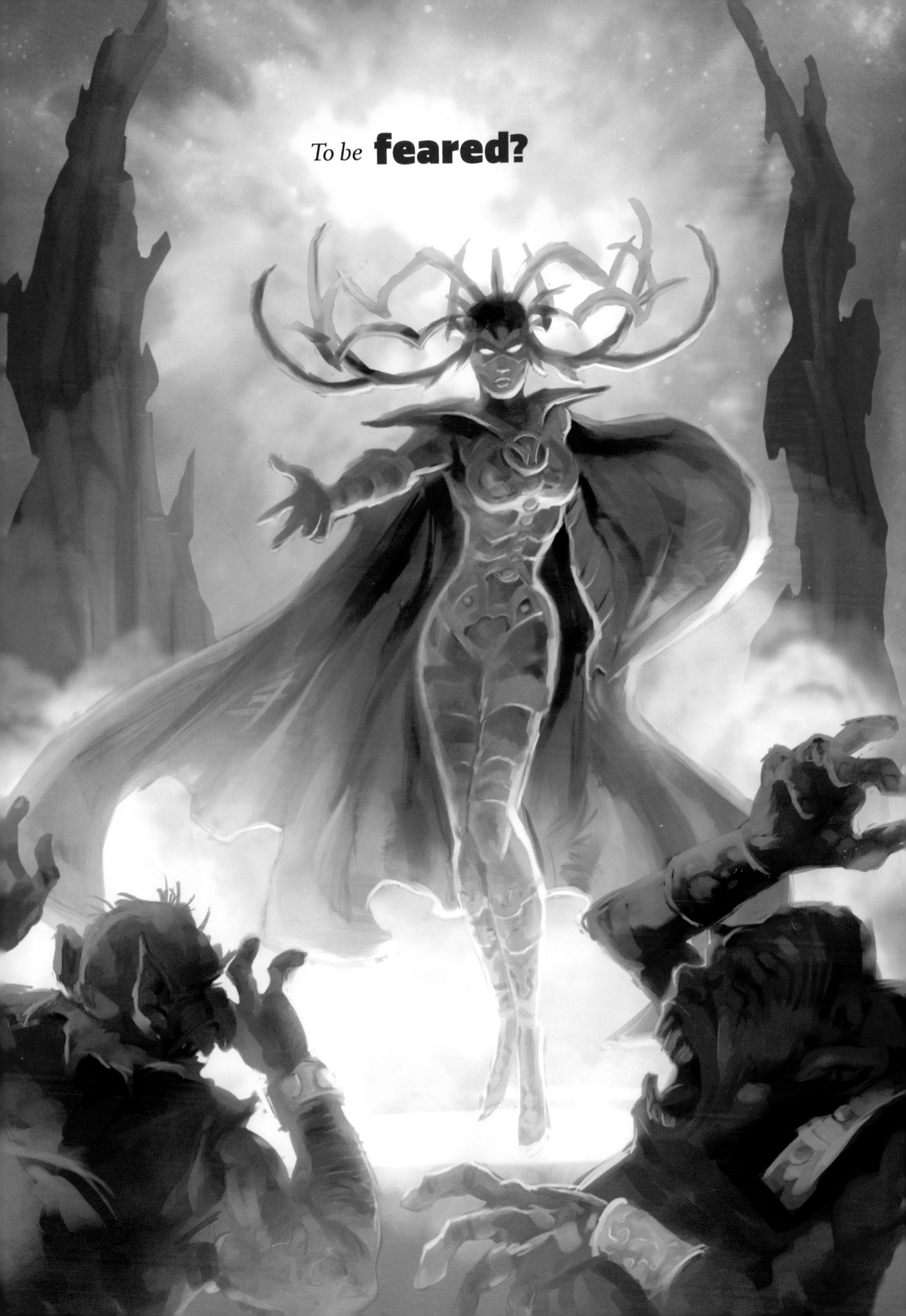
To be **feared?**

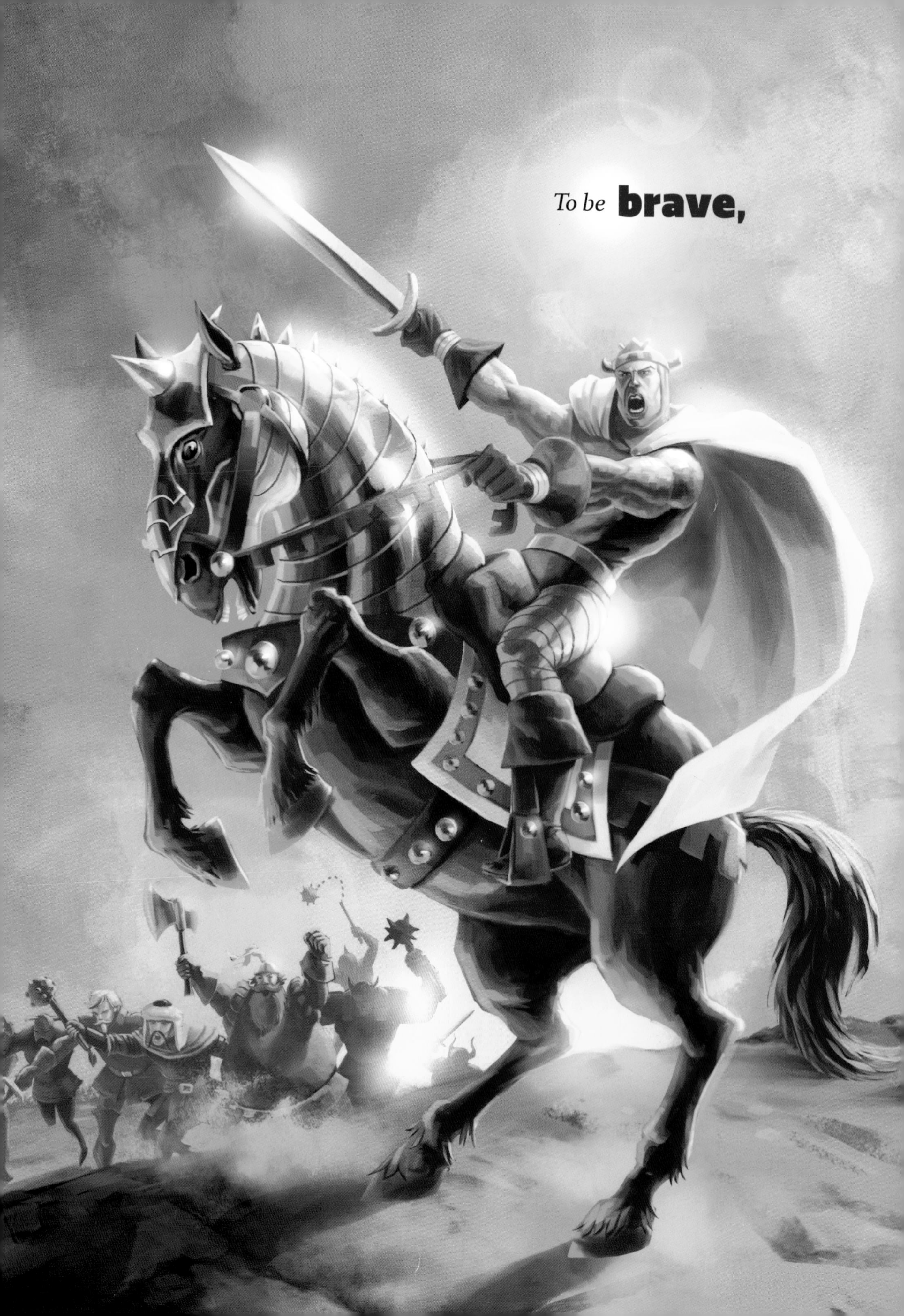

To be **brave,**

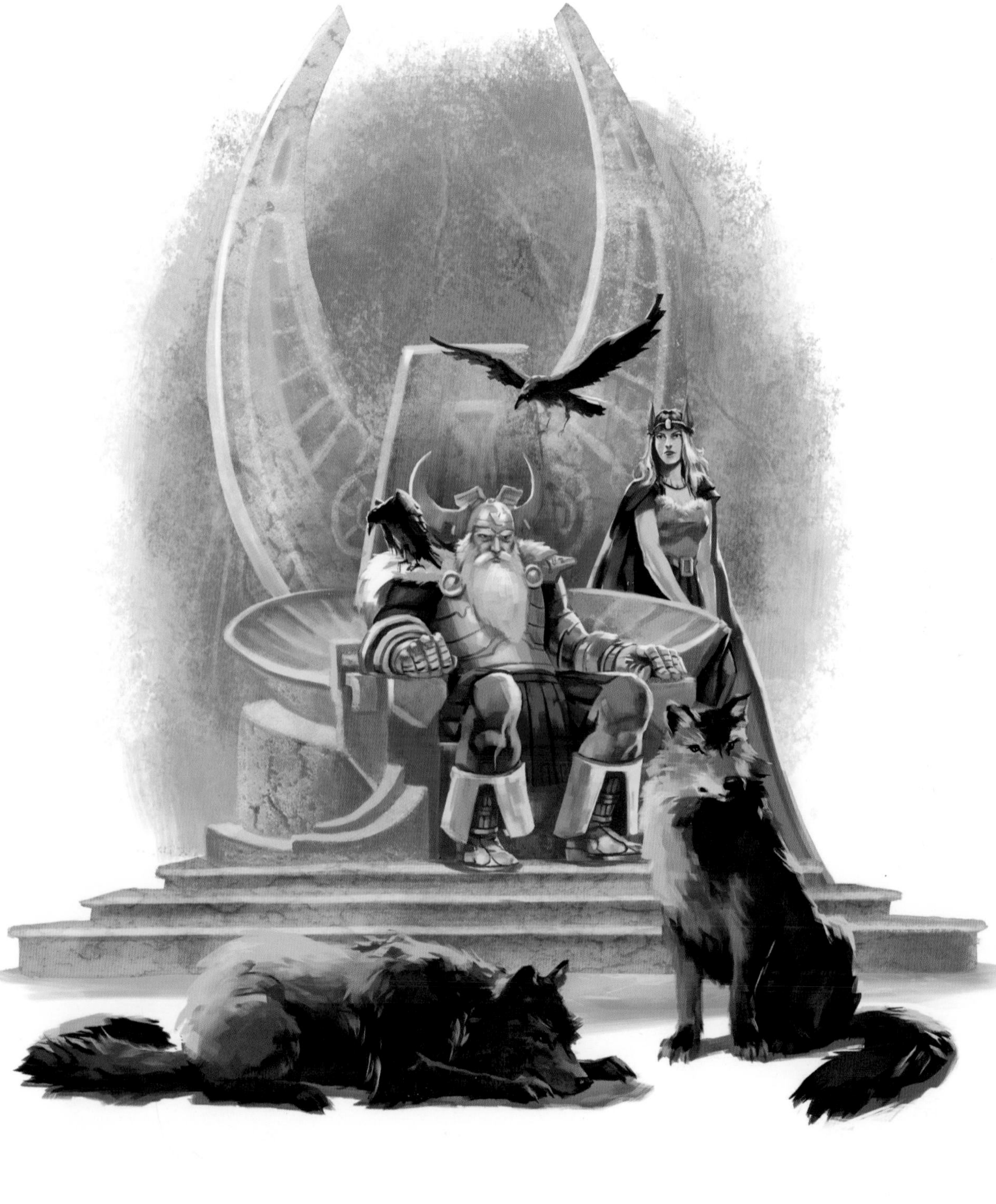

to be **honored—**

to be **MIGHTY?**

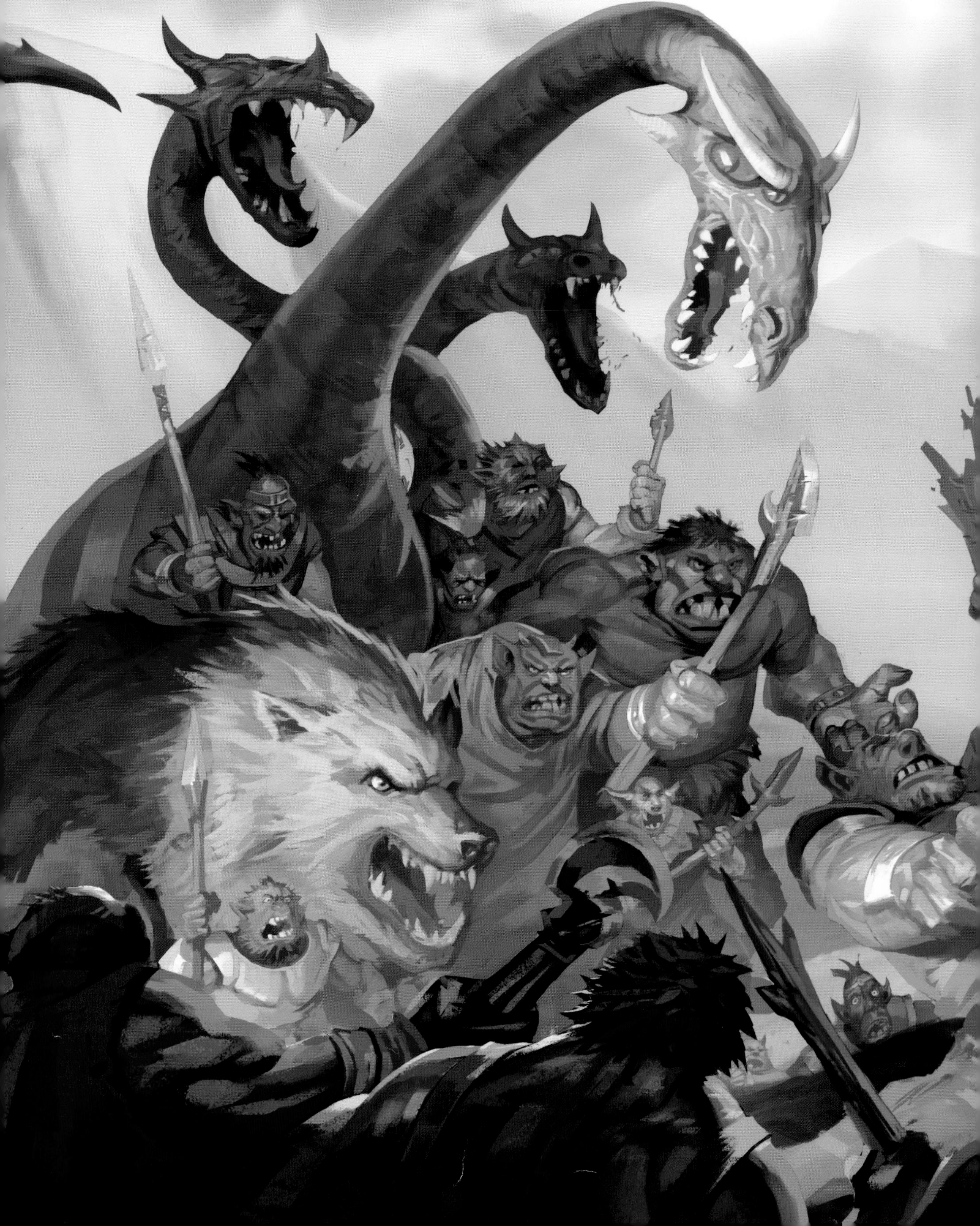

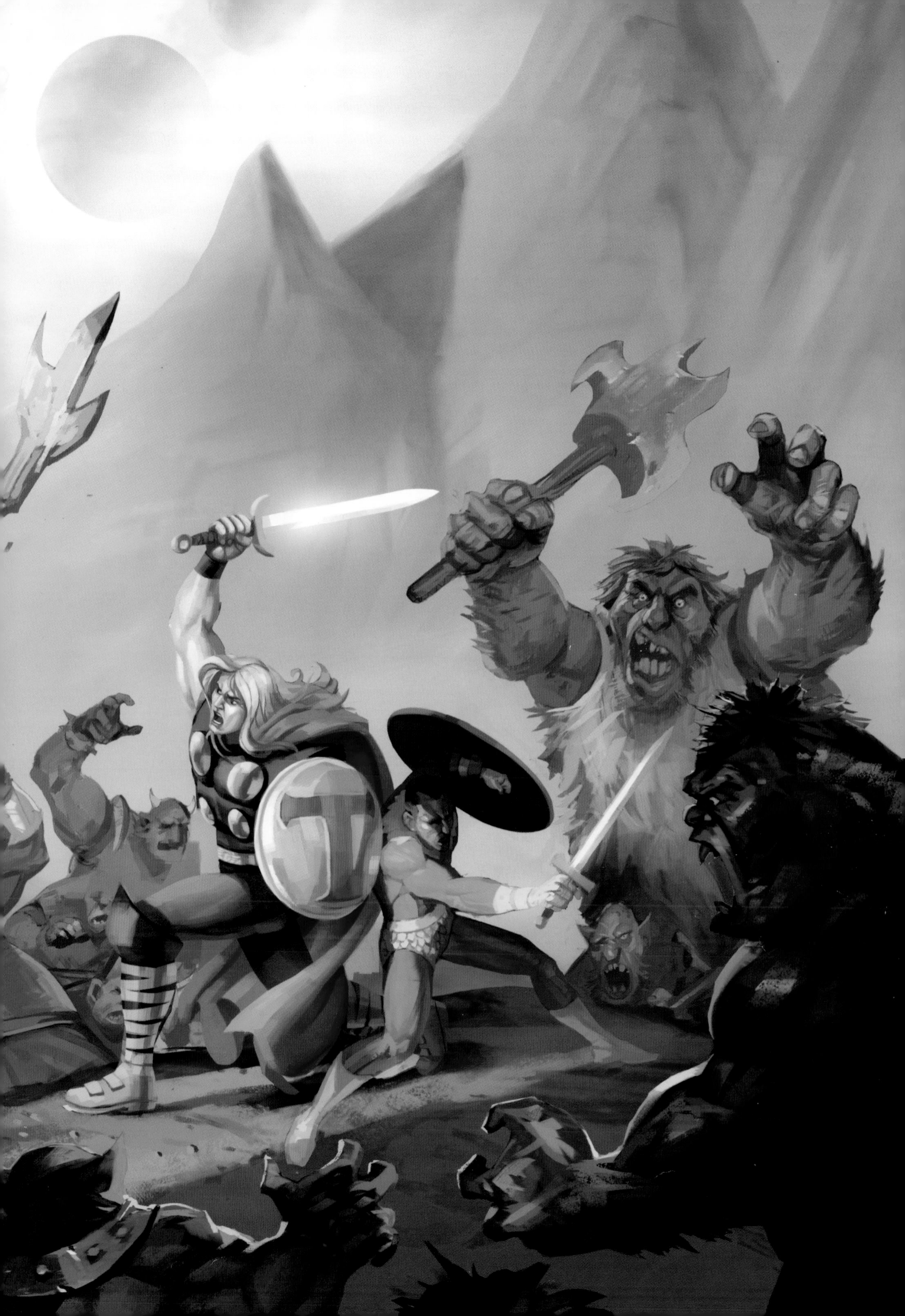

Some are **born** with these qualities.

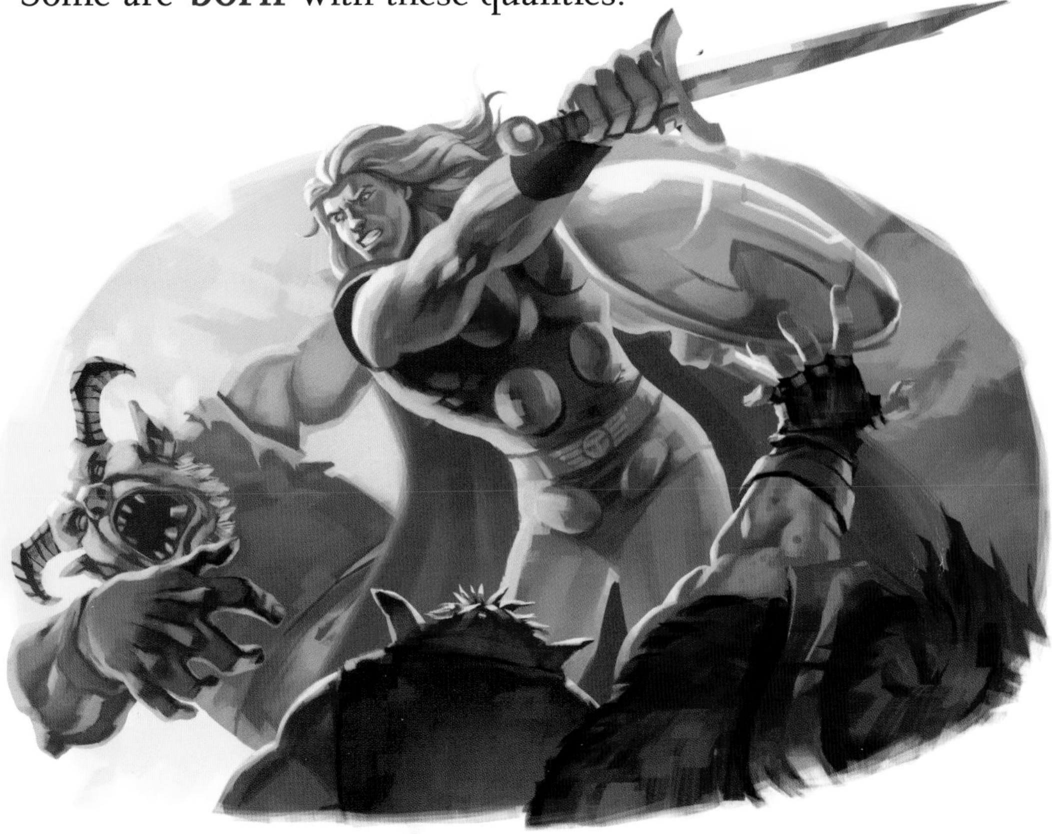

And some spend their lives **working** to attain them.

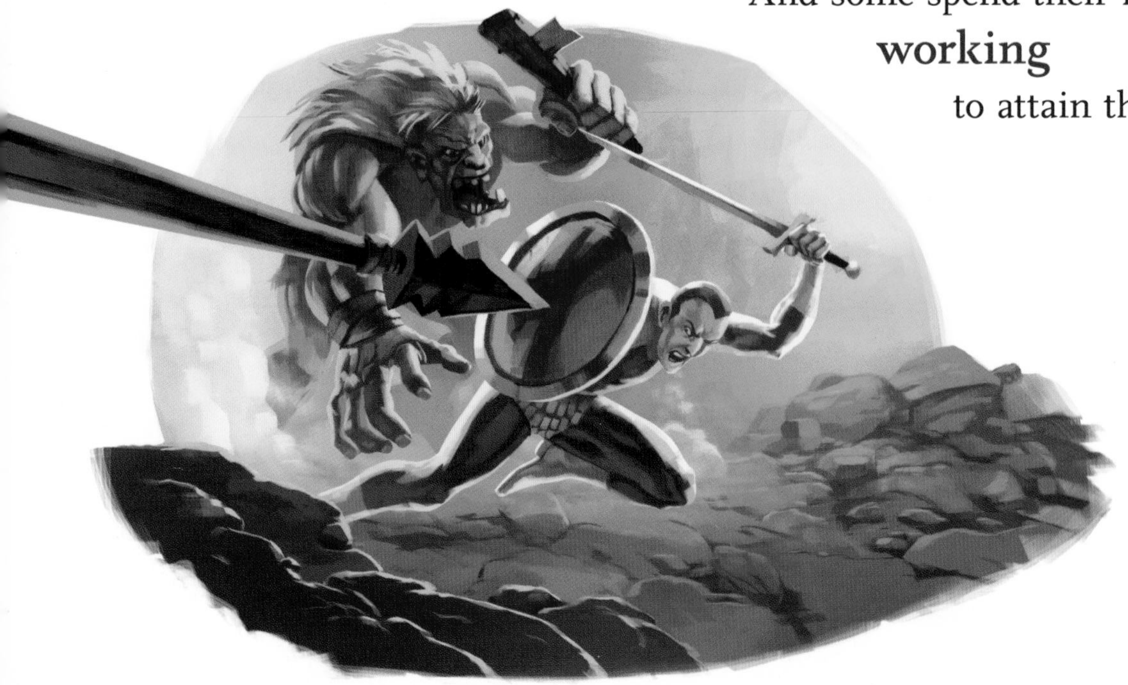

This is a story about someone who was born into royalty **but needed** **to *earn* his *honor.***

This is a story about a *hero*

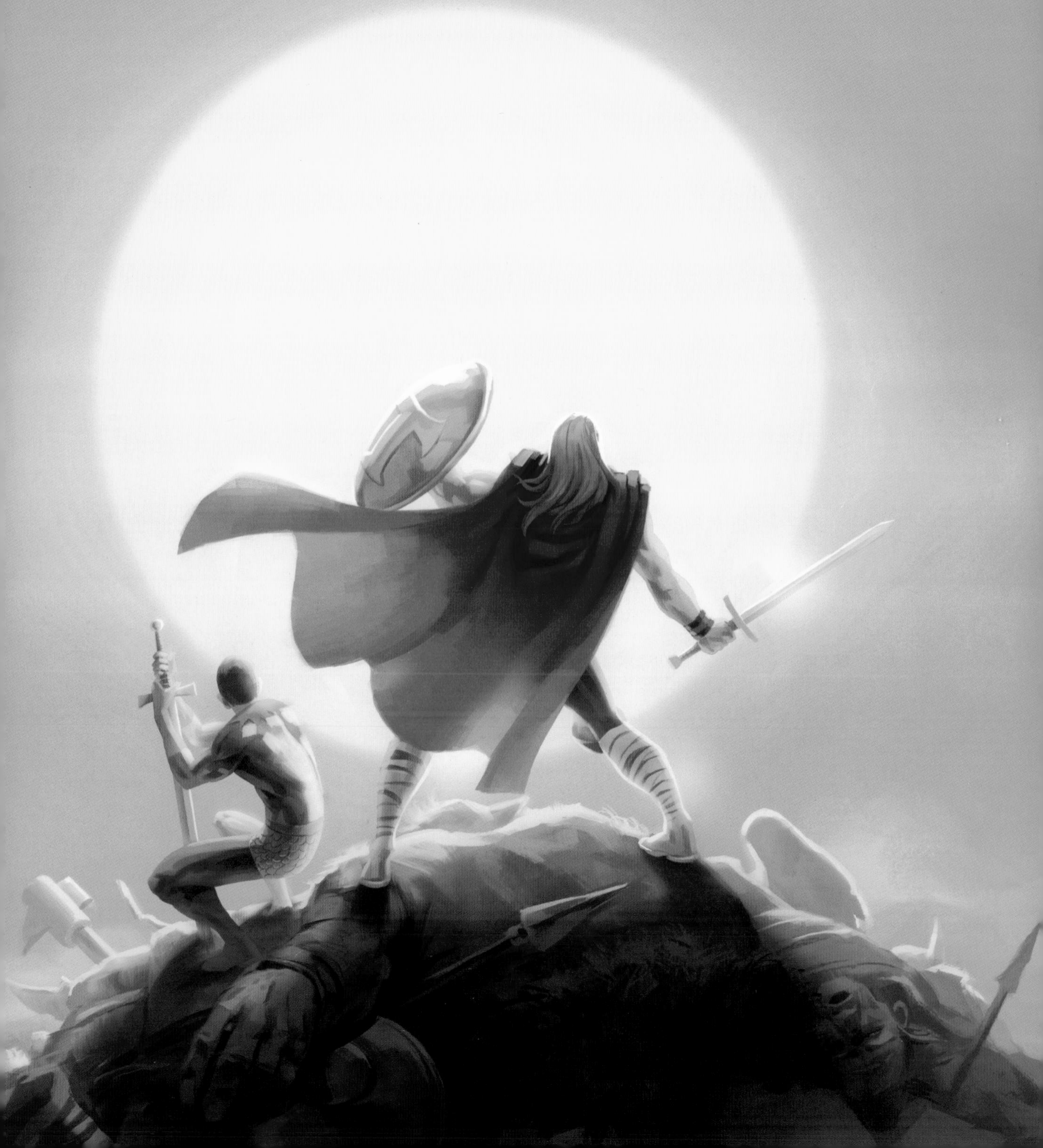

named **THOR.**

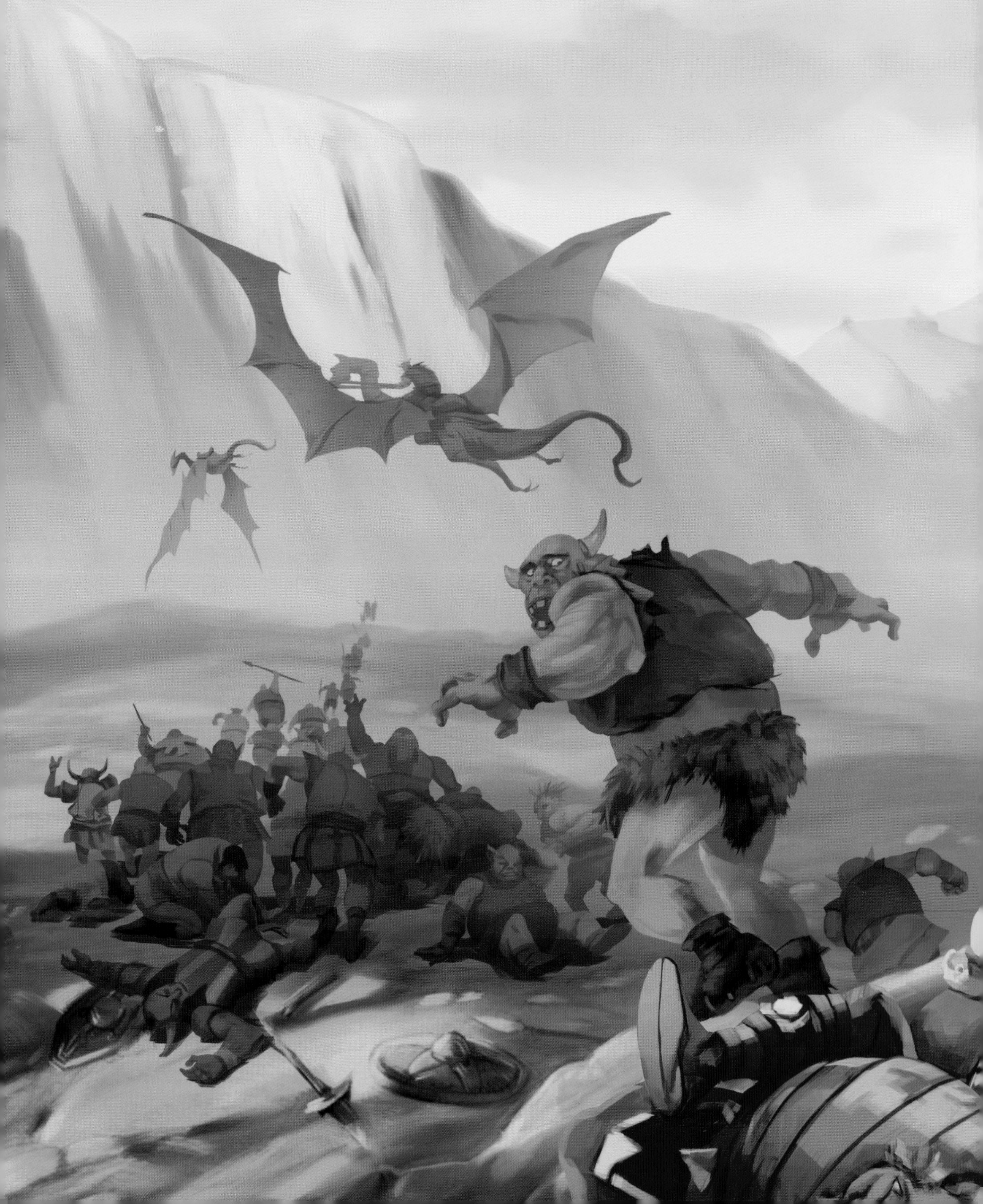

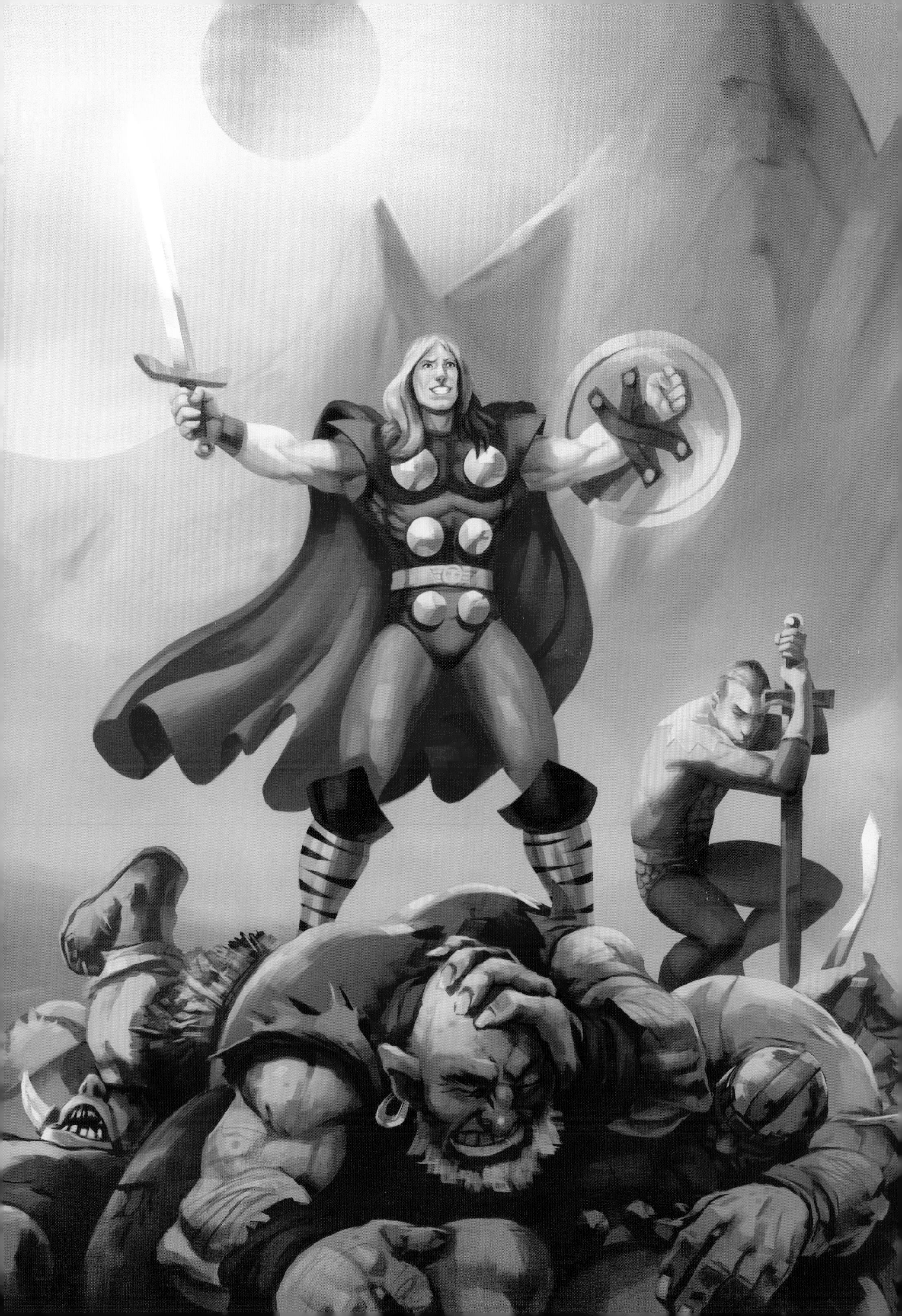

Thor's realm was called Asgard.
It sat like an island whose shores were
swept by the sea of space.

The people who lived on Asgard were called
Asgardians and the Asgardians called our
world *Midgard*. The only way to reach our
world from theirs was by the rainbow bridge,
Bifrost. The bridge was guarded by the
sentry called *Heimdall*.

Even though Asgard was well-protected,
threats were endless.

Thor was one of the land's
great protectors.

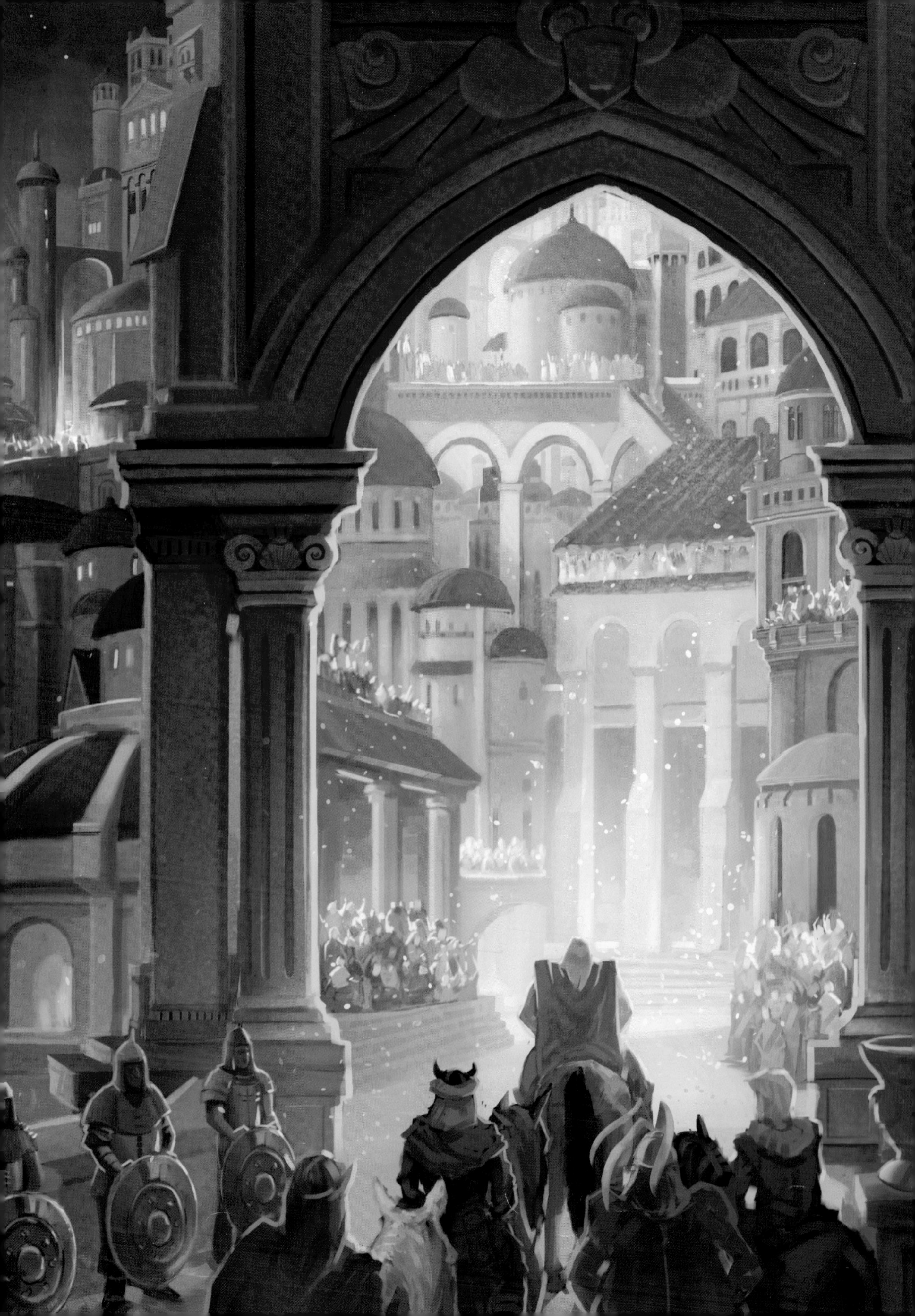

He was also a prince. He lived with his brother Loki in the castle of their father, Odin.

Thor was arrogant and chose his friends for their loyalty: the brave warrior Balder, and a band of soldiers called the Warriors Three—Fandral, Volstagg, and Hogun—and the beautiful, strong, and wise Lady Sif.

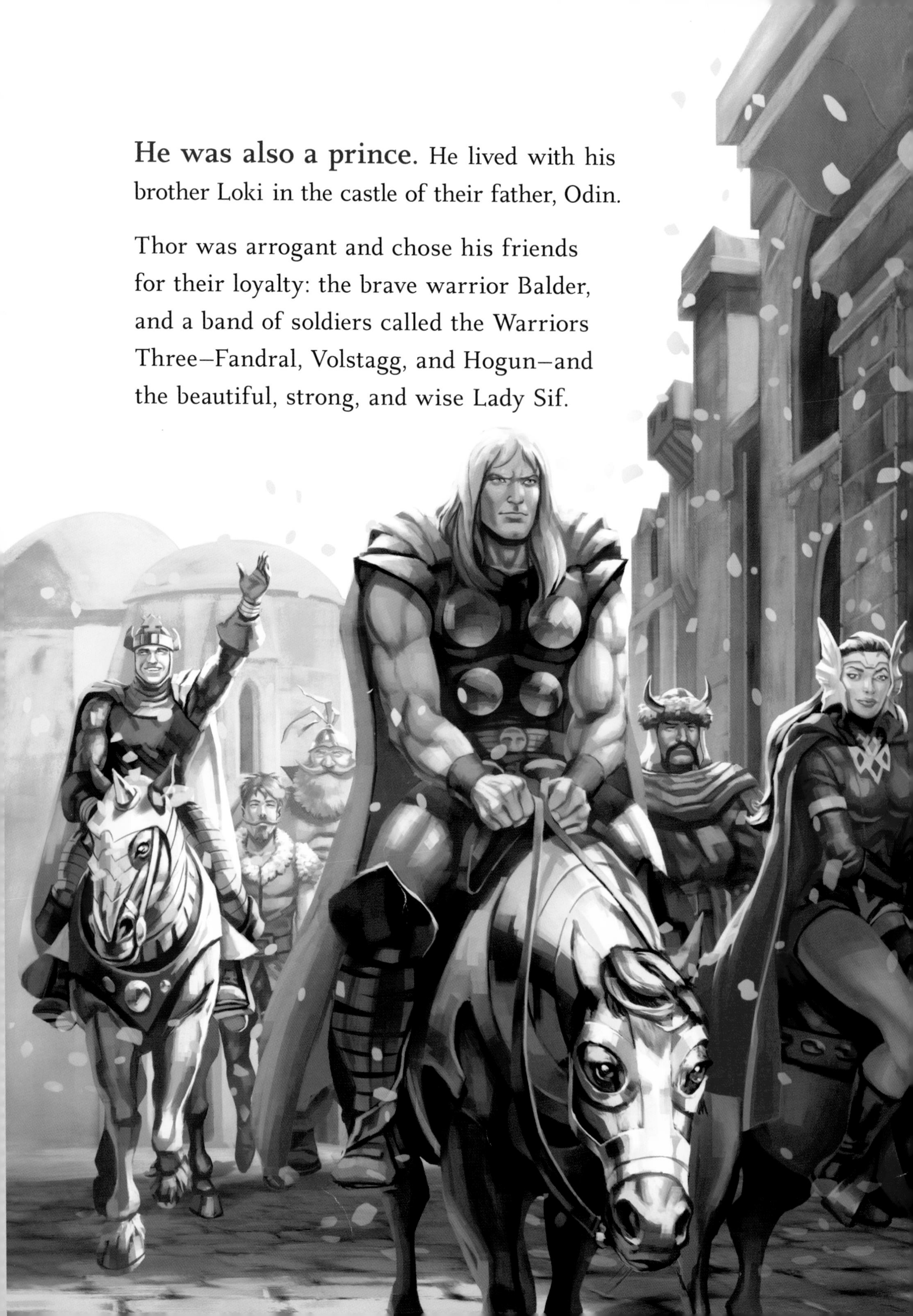

Thor's father, Odin, ruled over all of Asgard.

He and his wife, Frigga, wanted nothing more than for their sons to grow up to be worthy rulers.

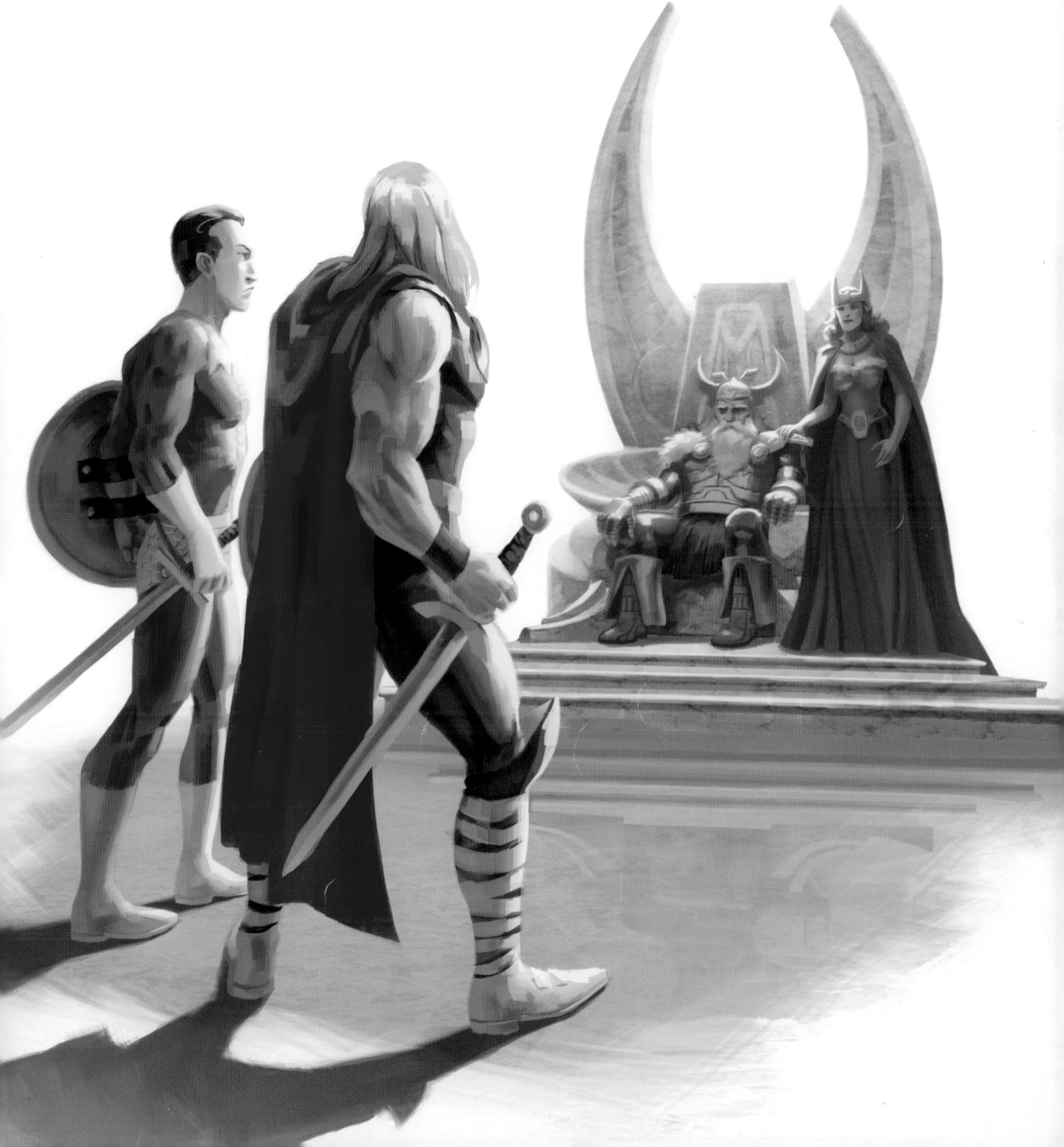

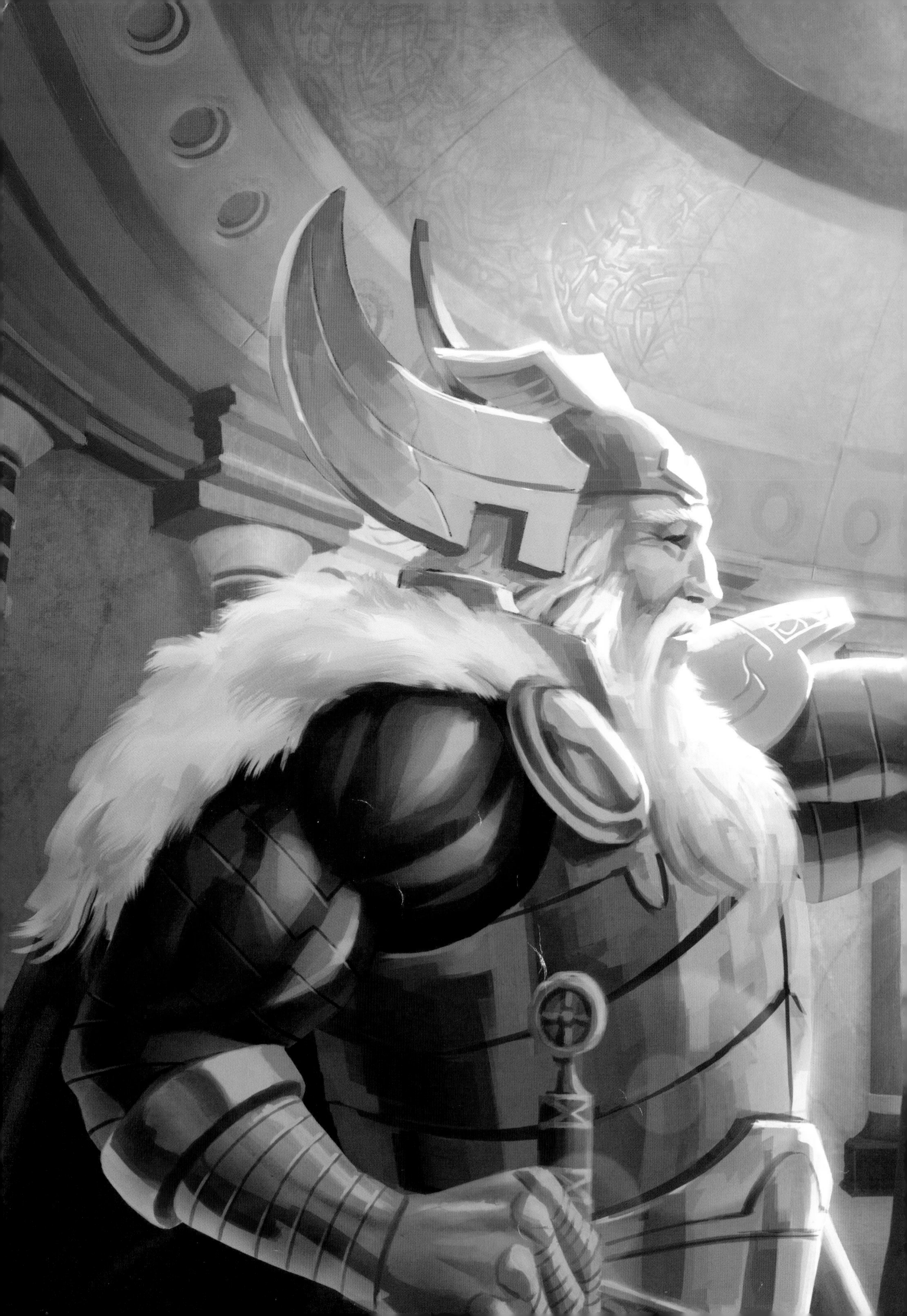

But there could only be one supreme ruler of Asgard. Only one who could be like Odin. And even though Loki was thoughtful, clever, and quick . . .

Thor was **first born**, and so the throne *was his* by right.

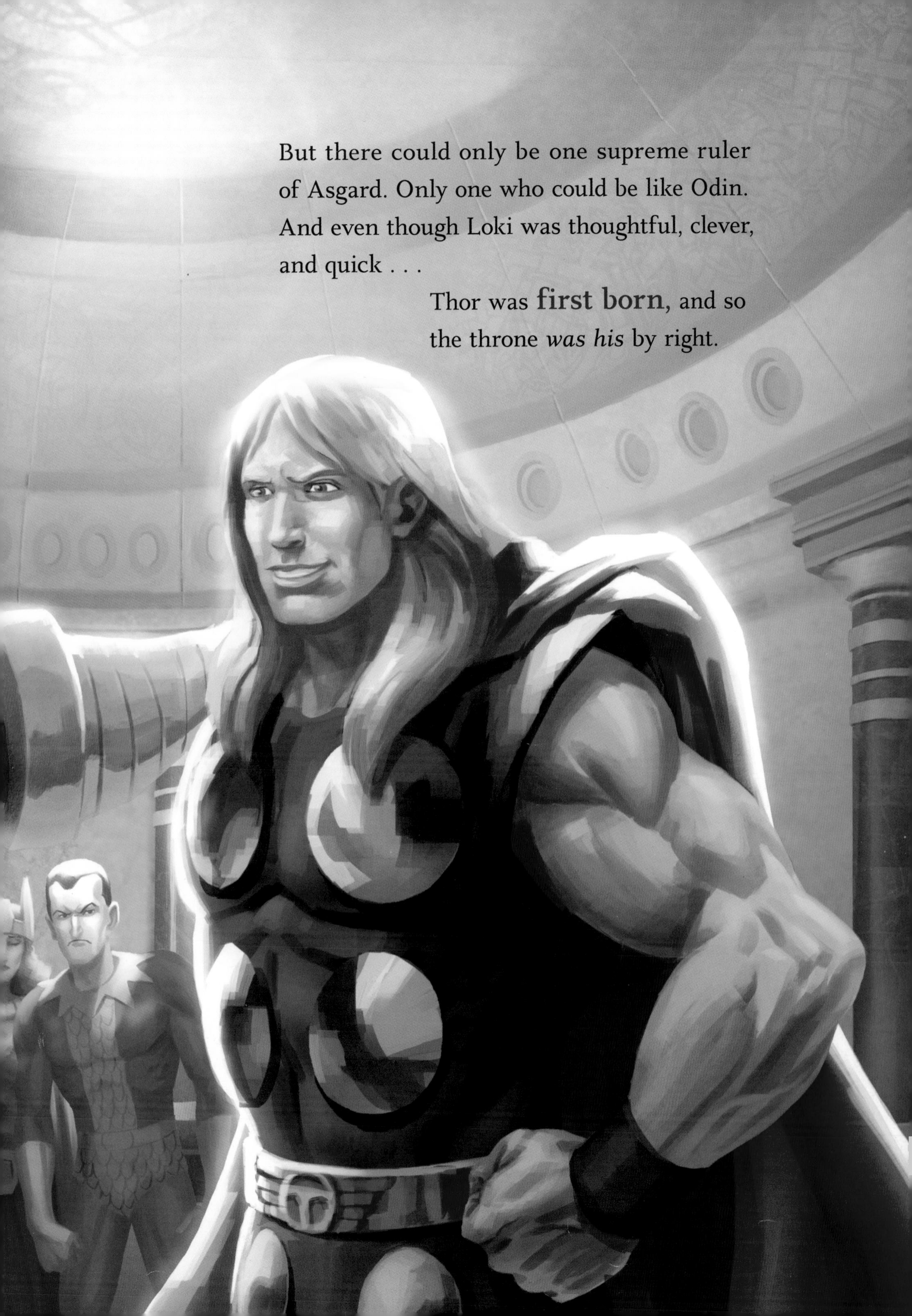

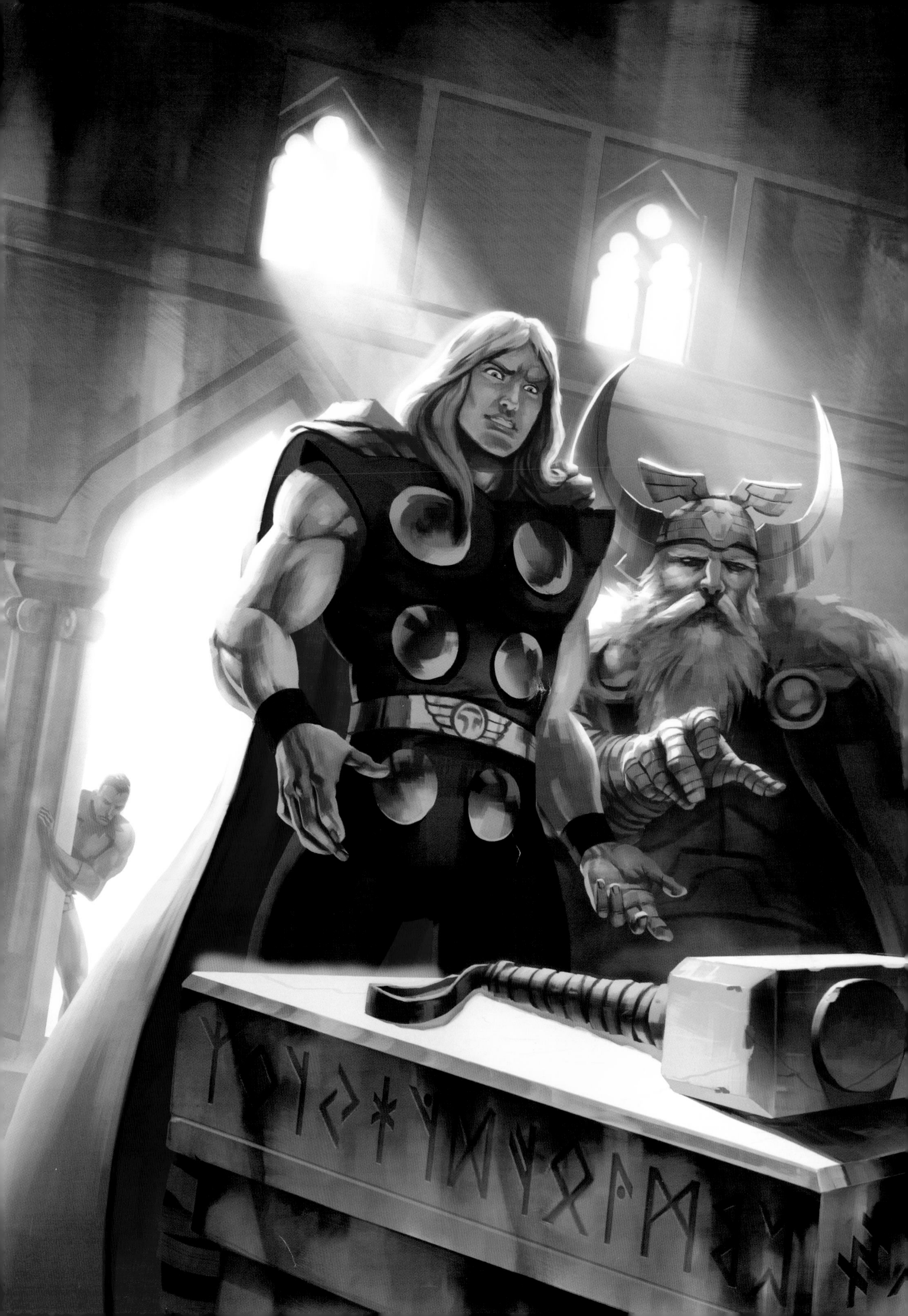

To determine when Thor would be ready to rule, Odin had a special hammer made. It was forged from a mystical metal called *Uru*, which came from the heart of a dying star.

The hammer was named . . .

Mjolnir, and it held **great power.**

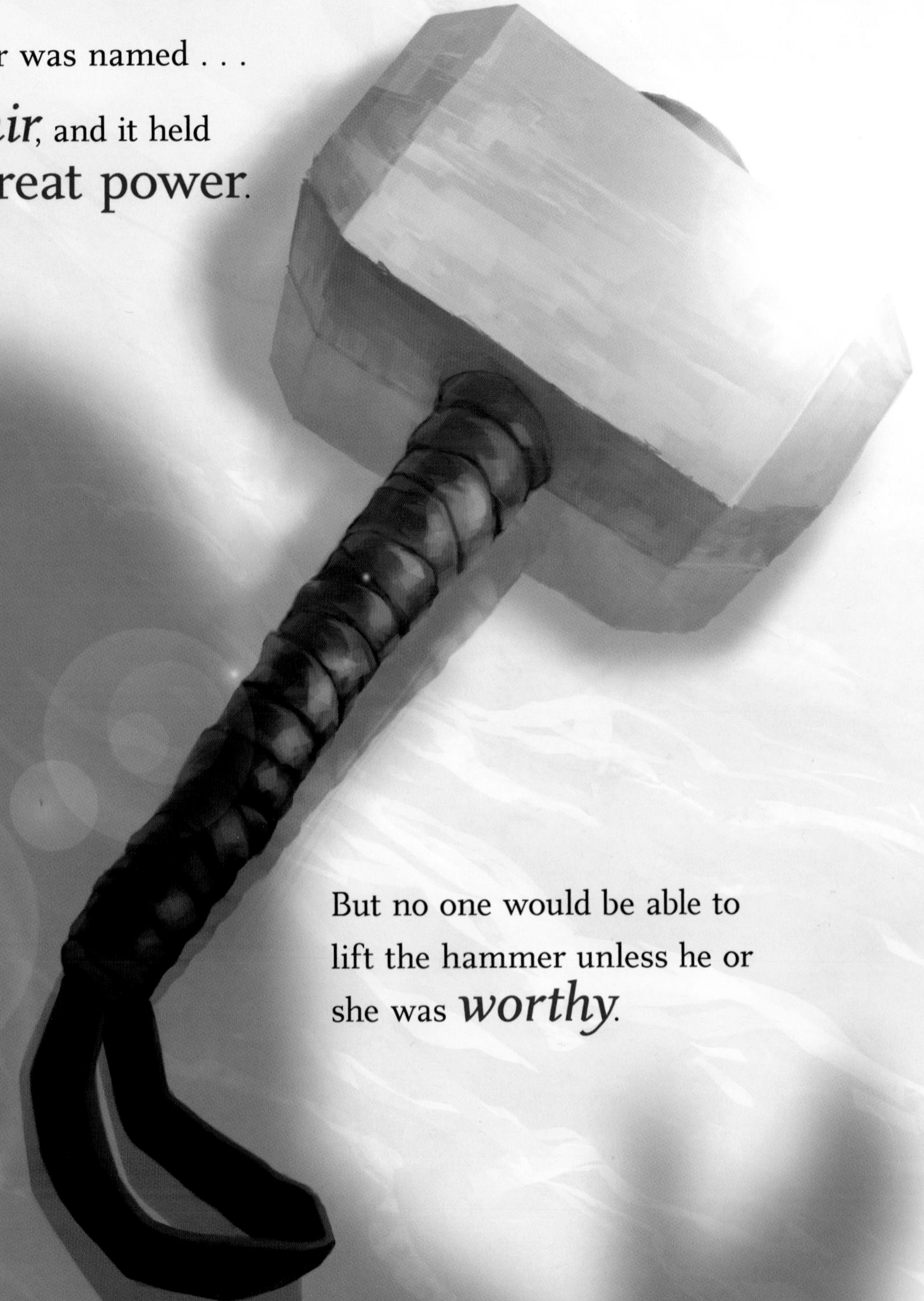

But no one would be able to lift the hammer unless he or she was *worthy*.

The hammer was **immovable** to Thor.

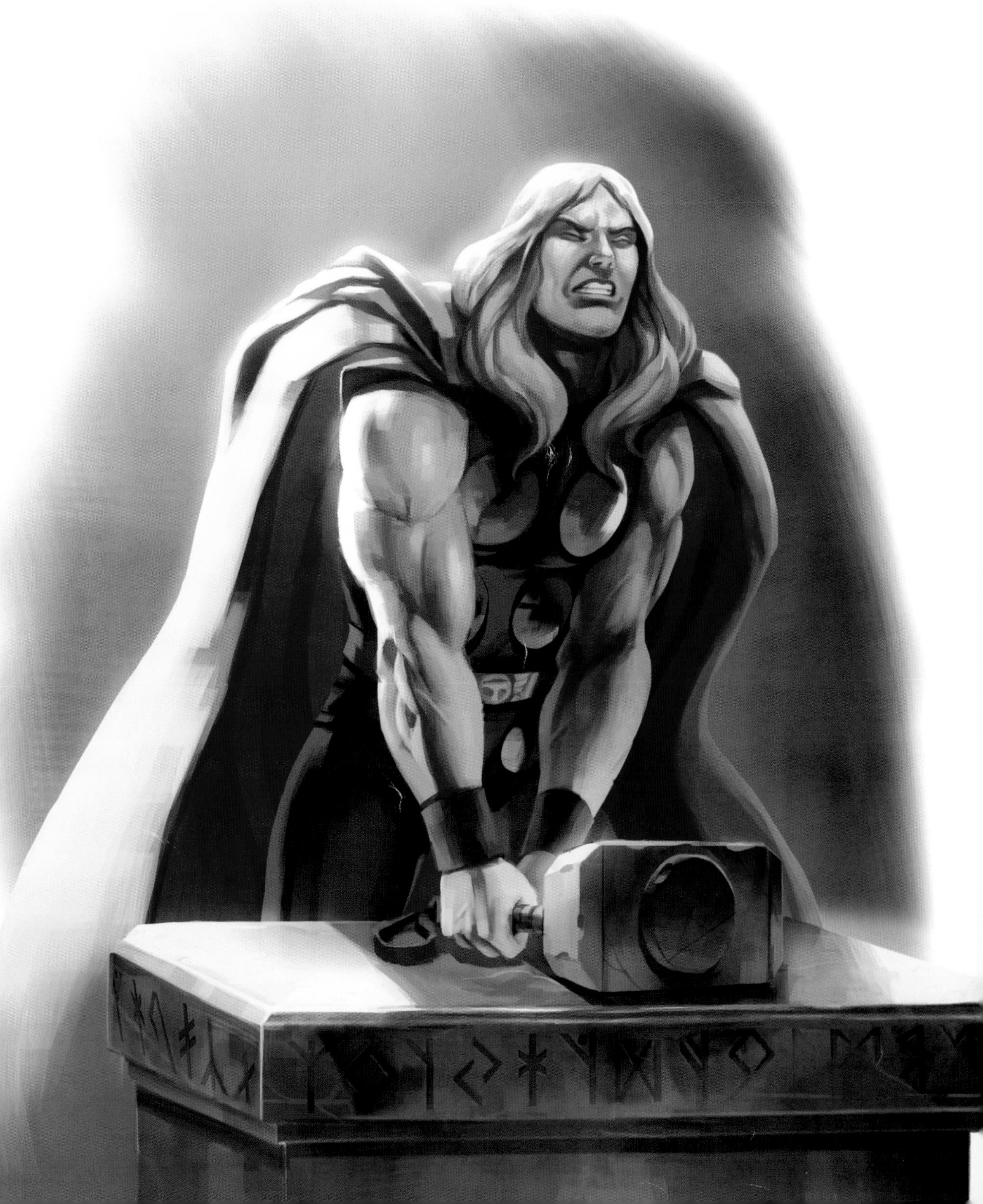

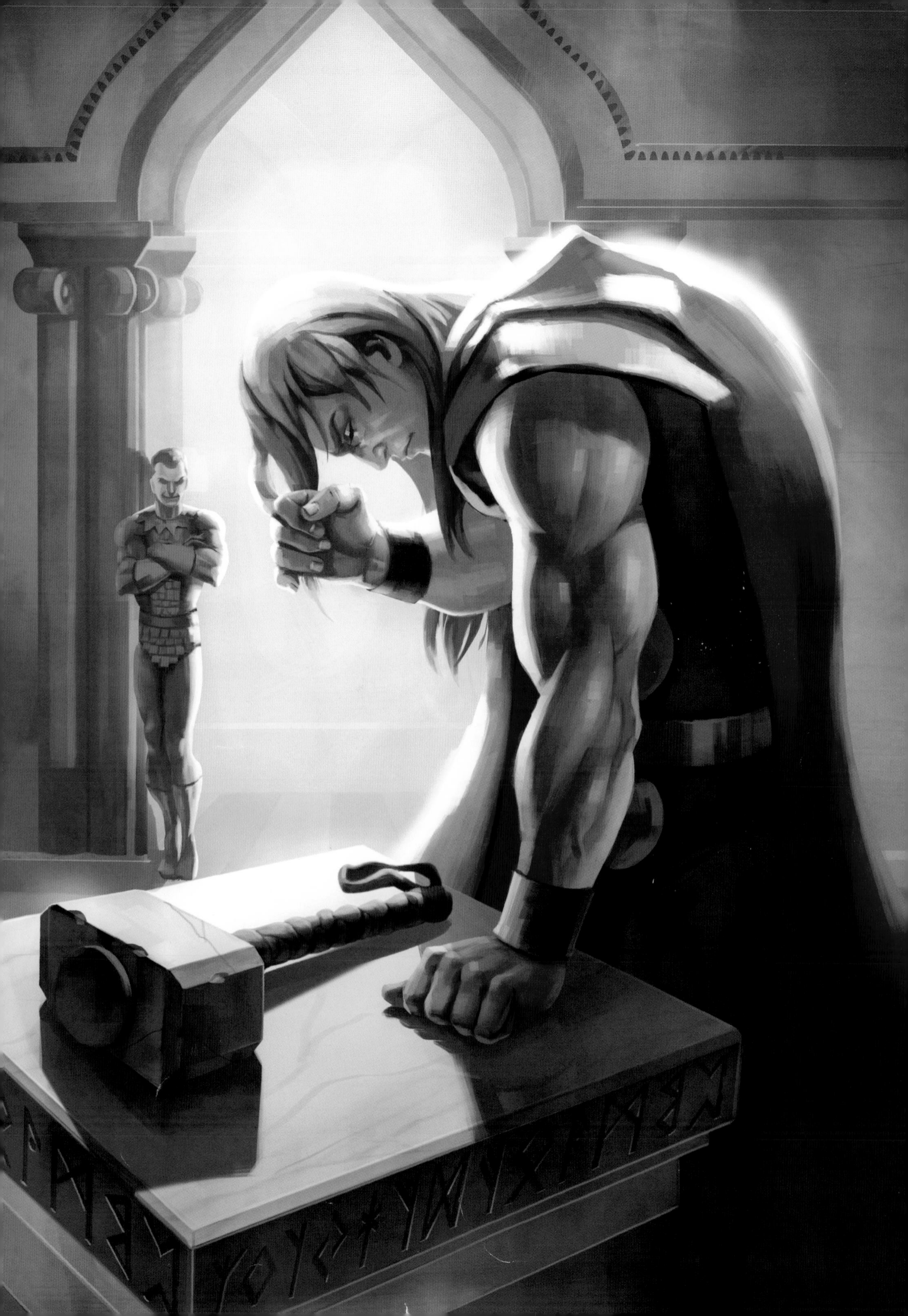

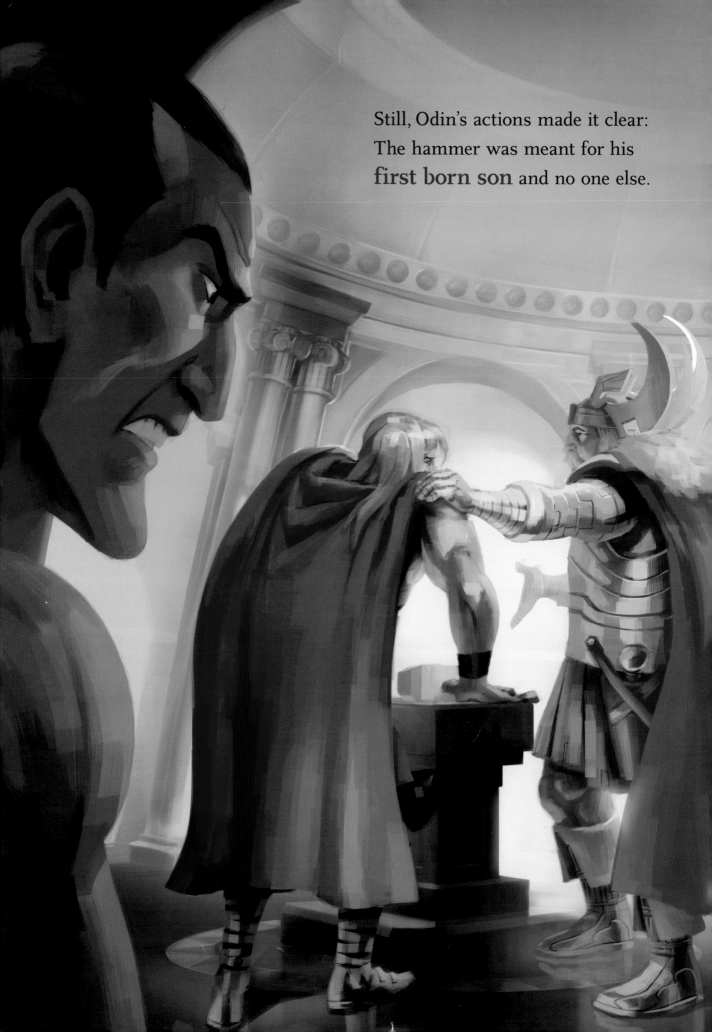

Still, Odin's actions made it clear:
The hammer was meant for his
first born son and no one else.

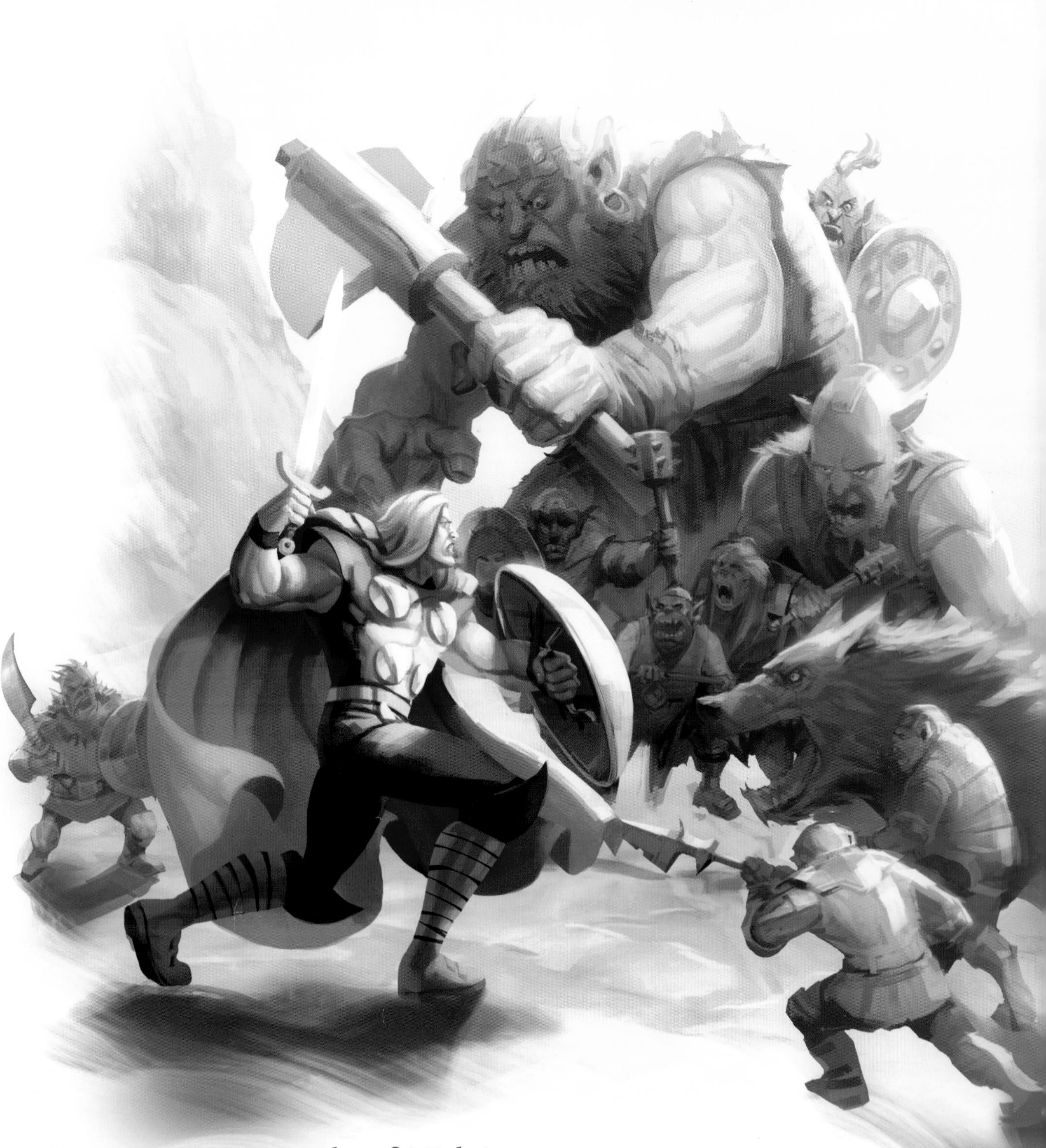

Even so, proving worthy of Mjolnir was not an easy task.

Thor spent nearly every moment trying to earn his right to hold the hammer.

He performed amazing acts of **bravery,**

he was honored
for acts of
nobility,

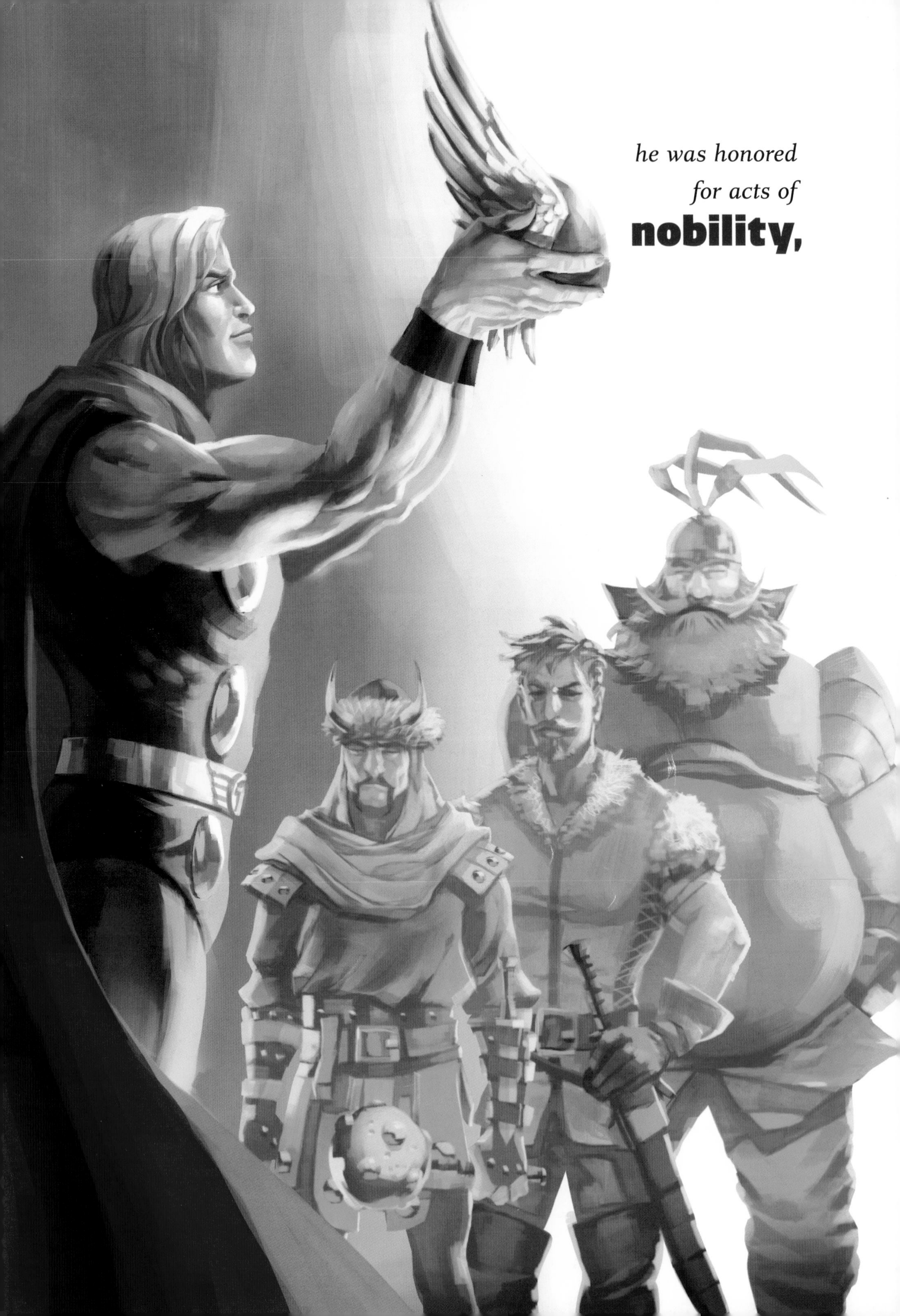

and he demonstrated
feats of great
strength

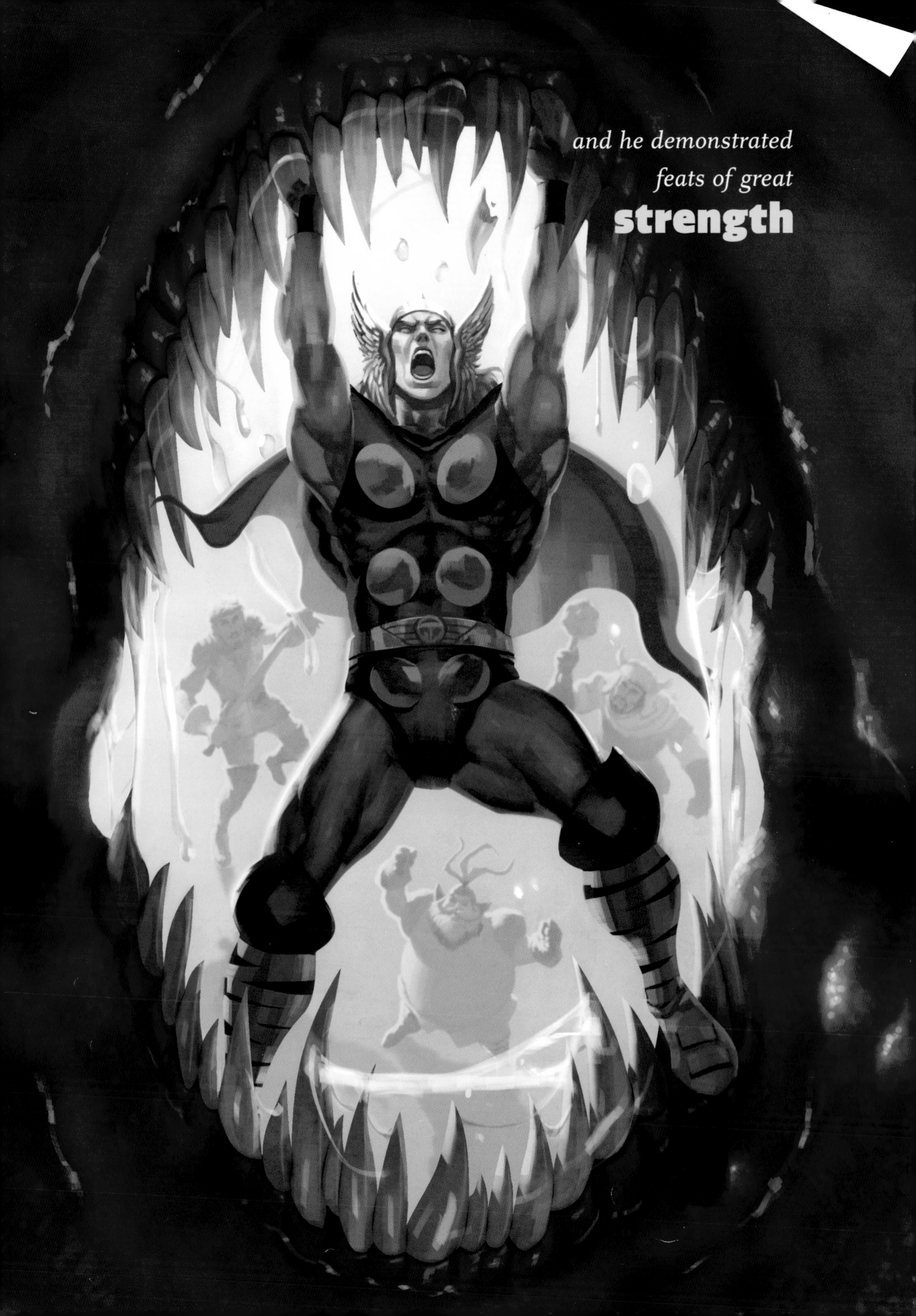

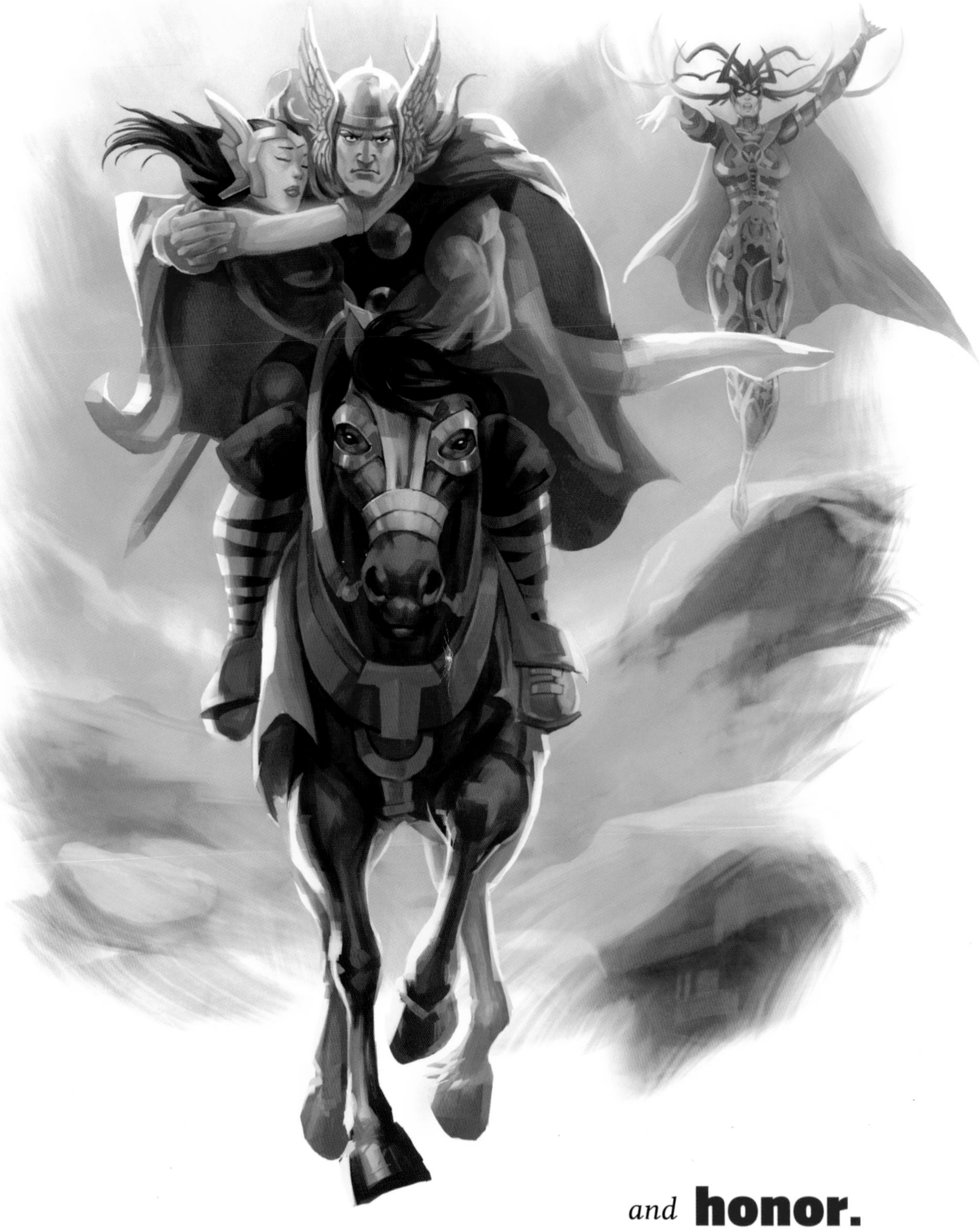

and **honor.**

With every great achievement, Thor attempted once more to pick up *Mjolnir.* It seemed as if he would never raise the hammer more than a few inches from the ground.

And then *one day . . .*

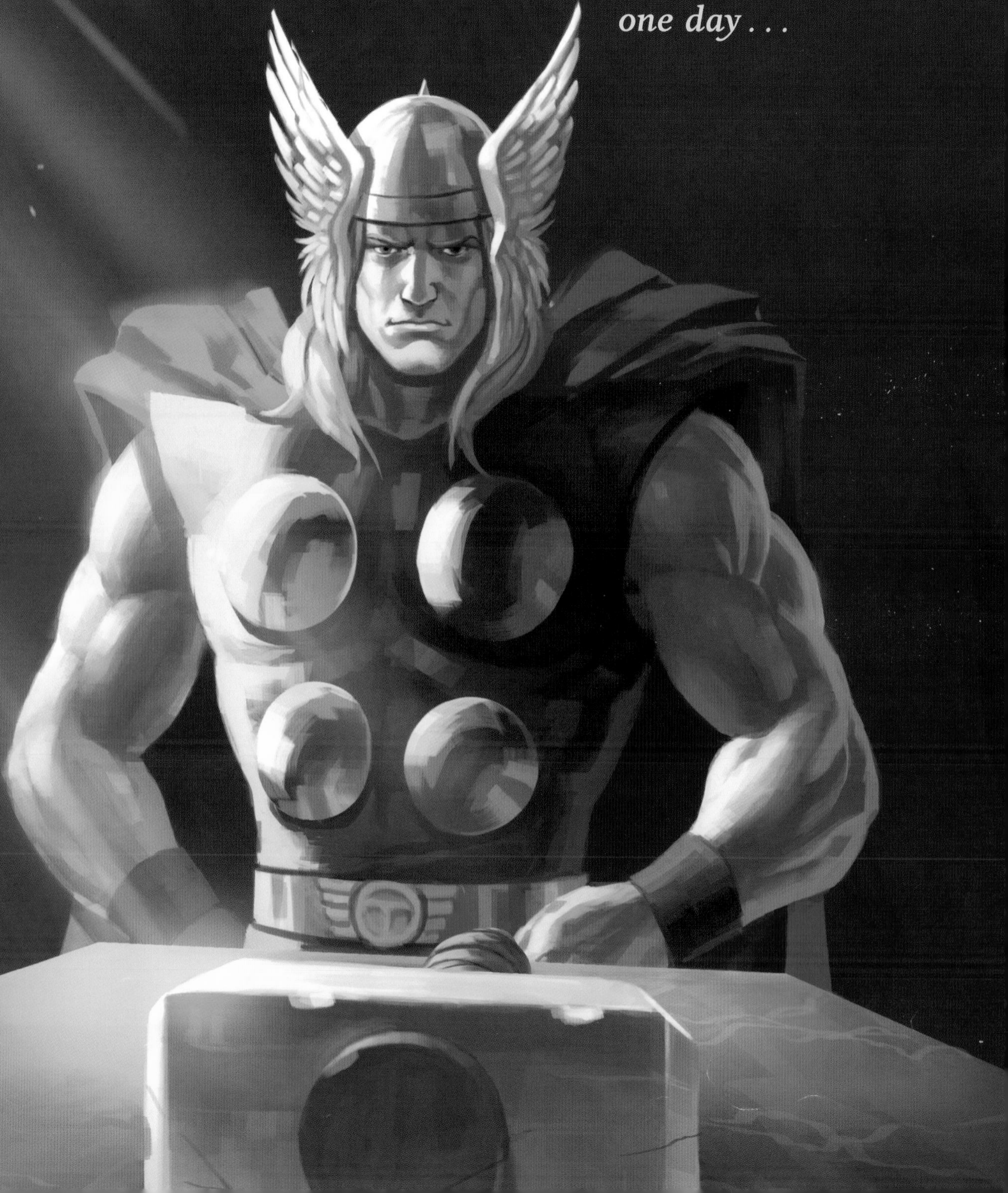

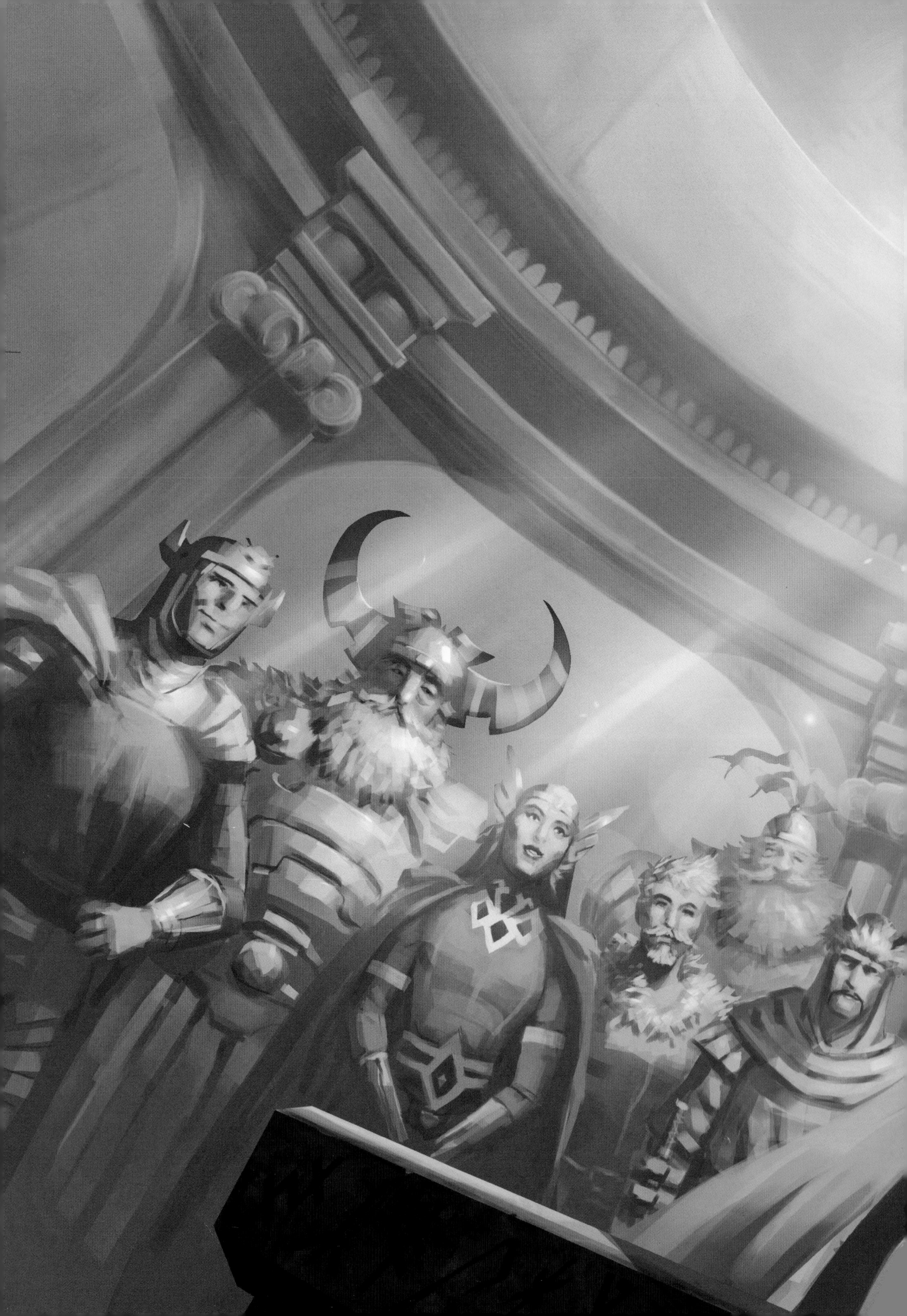

he **DID.**

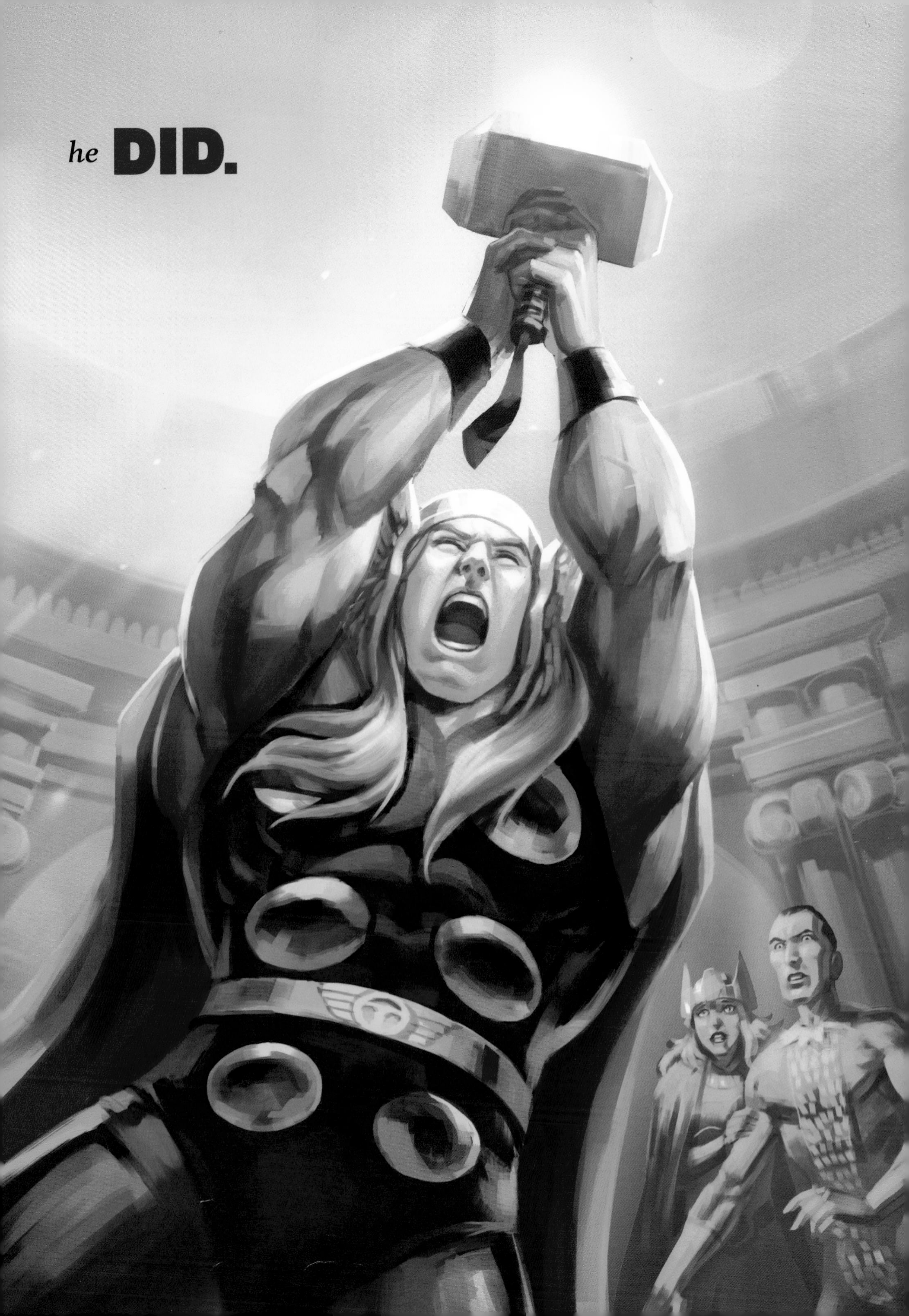

Thor had proven himself worthy of his weapon, and he used it well. When he threw the hammer, it always returned to him.

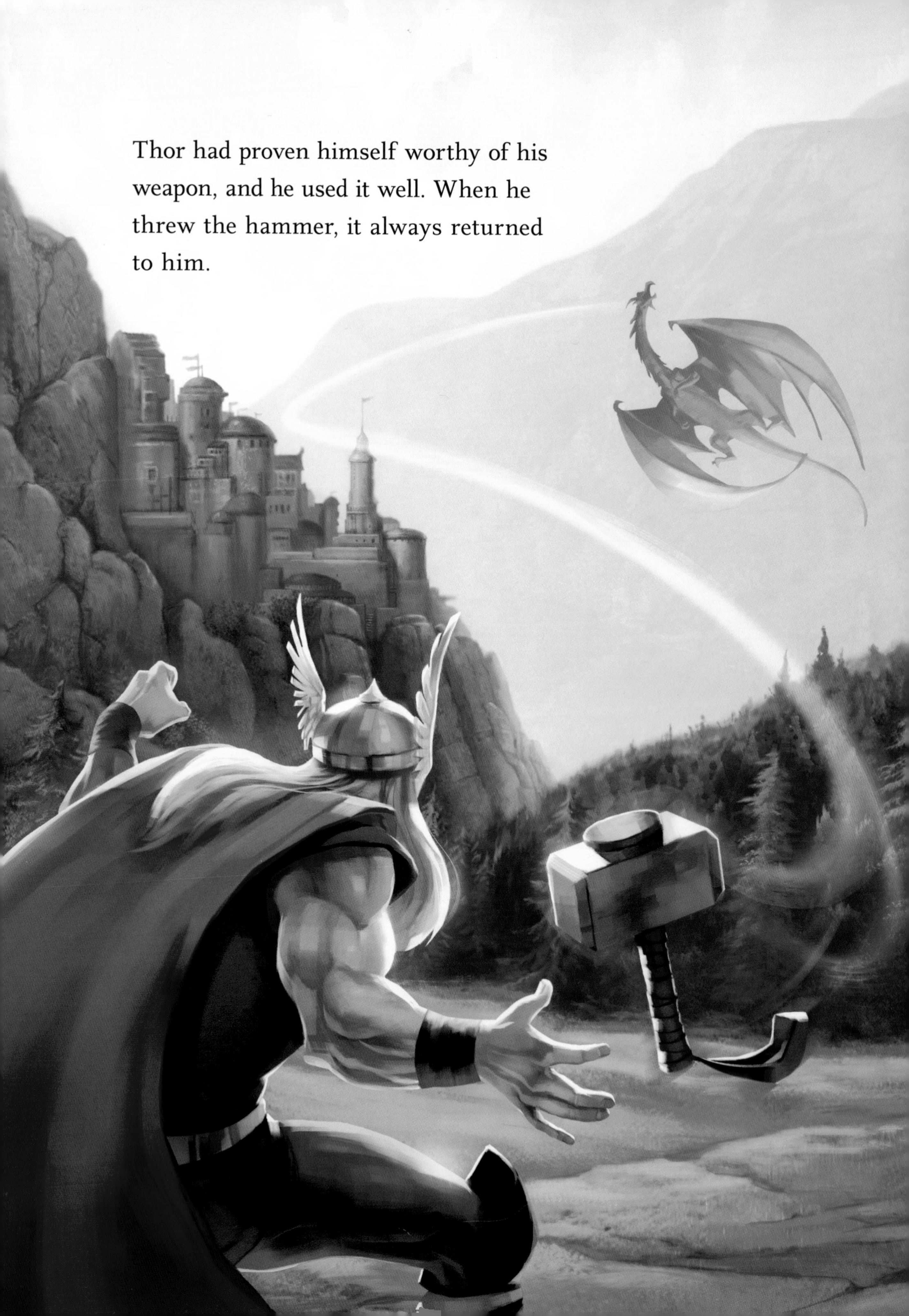

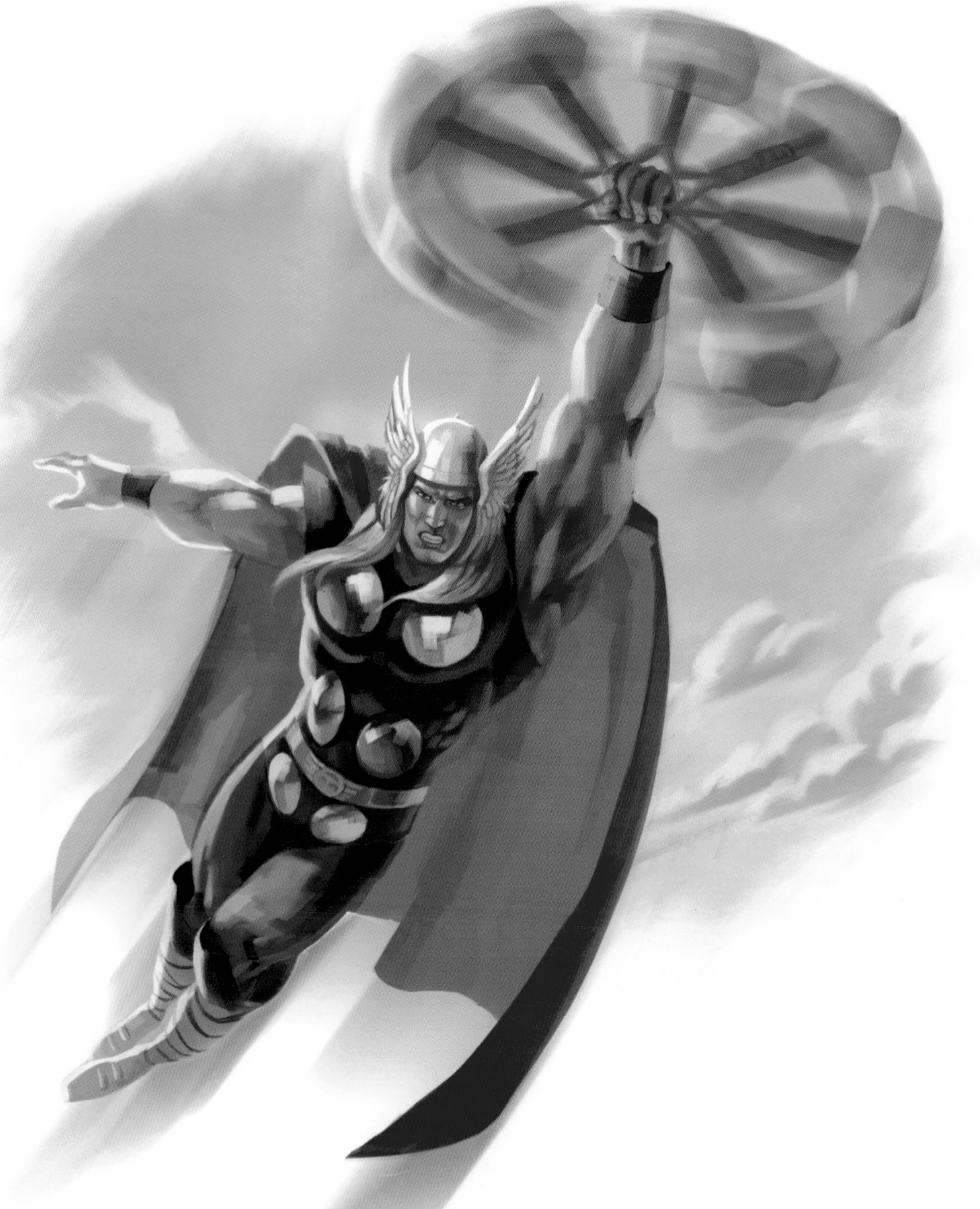

When he twirled it by its handle,
he could soar like a winged beast!

And when he stamped it ***twice***
upon the ground,

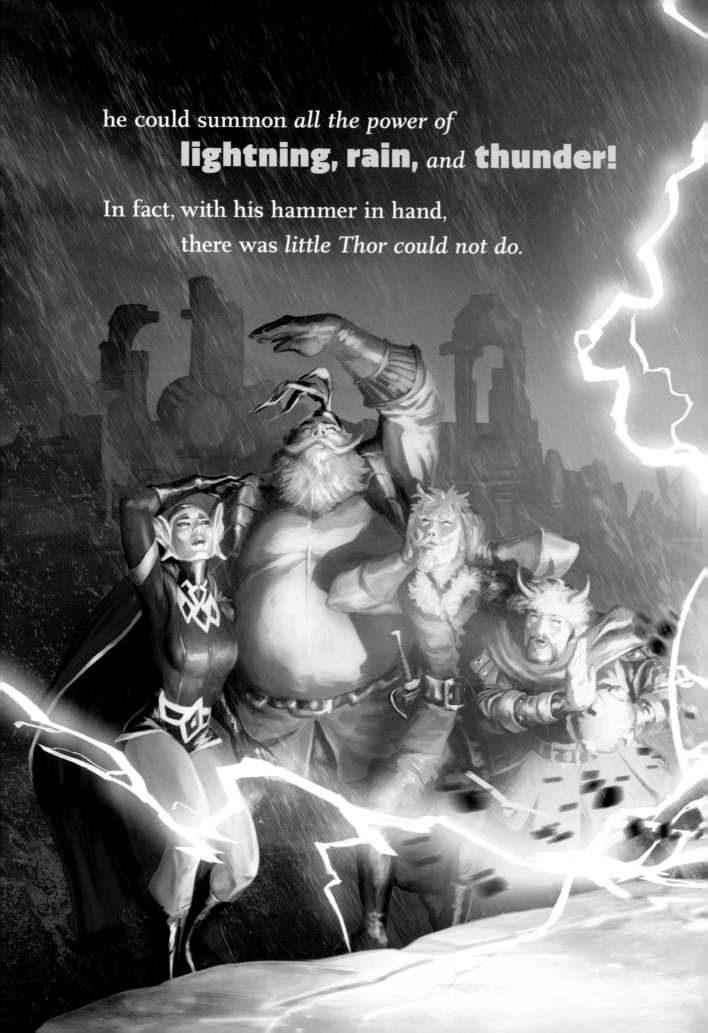

he could summon *all the power of* **lightning, rain,** *and* **thunder!**

In fact, with his hammer in hand,
there was *little Thor could not do.*

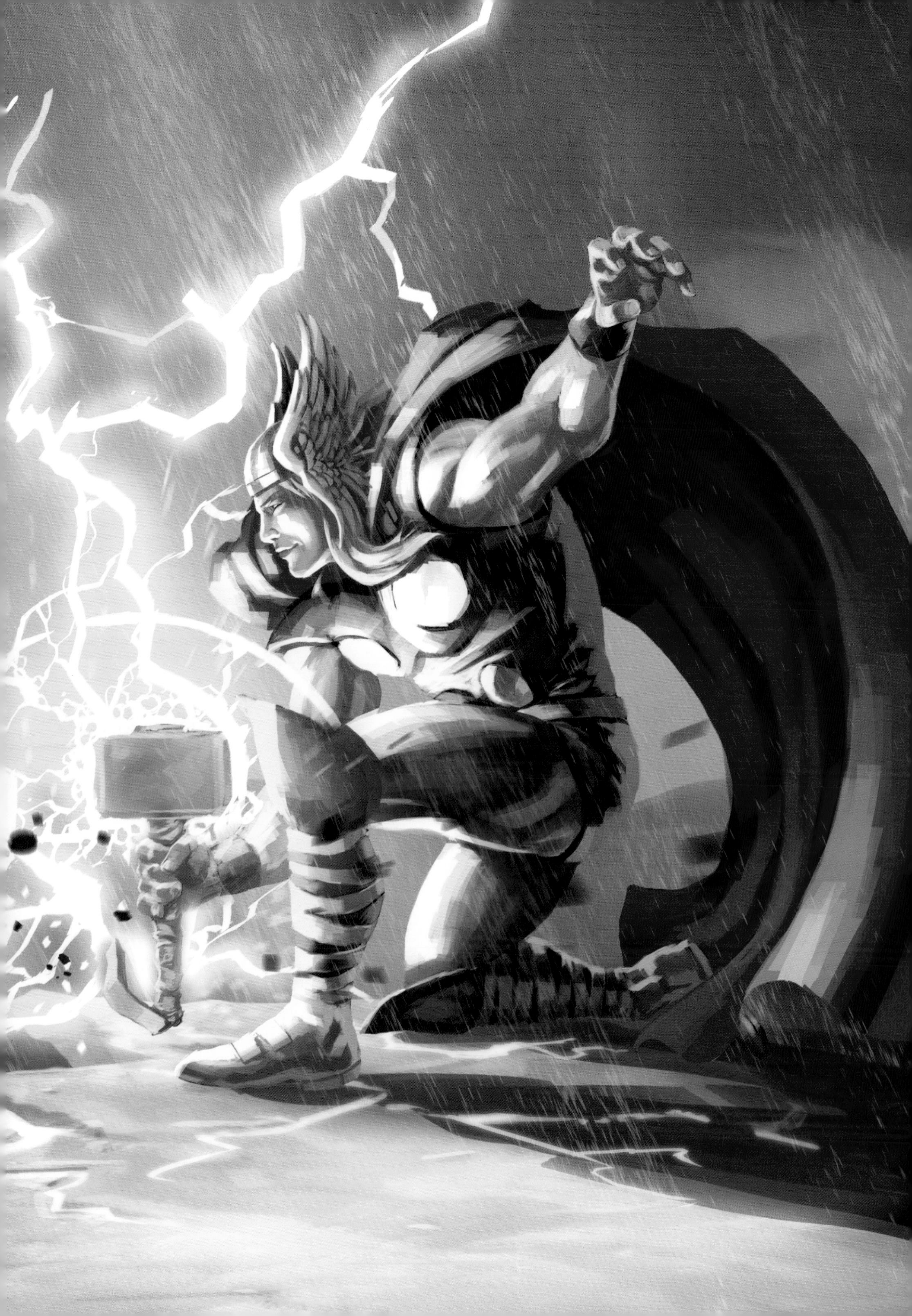

And he **knew** *it.*

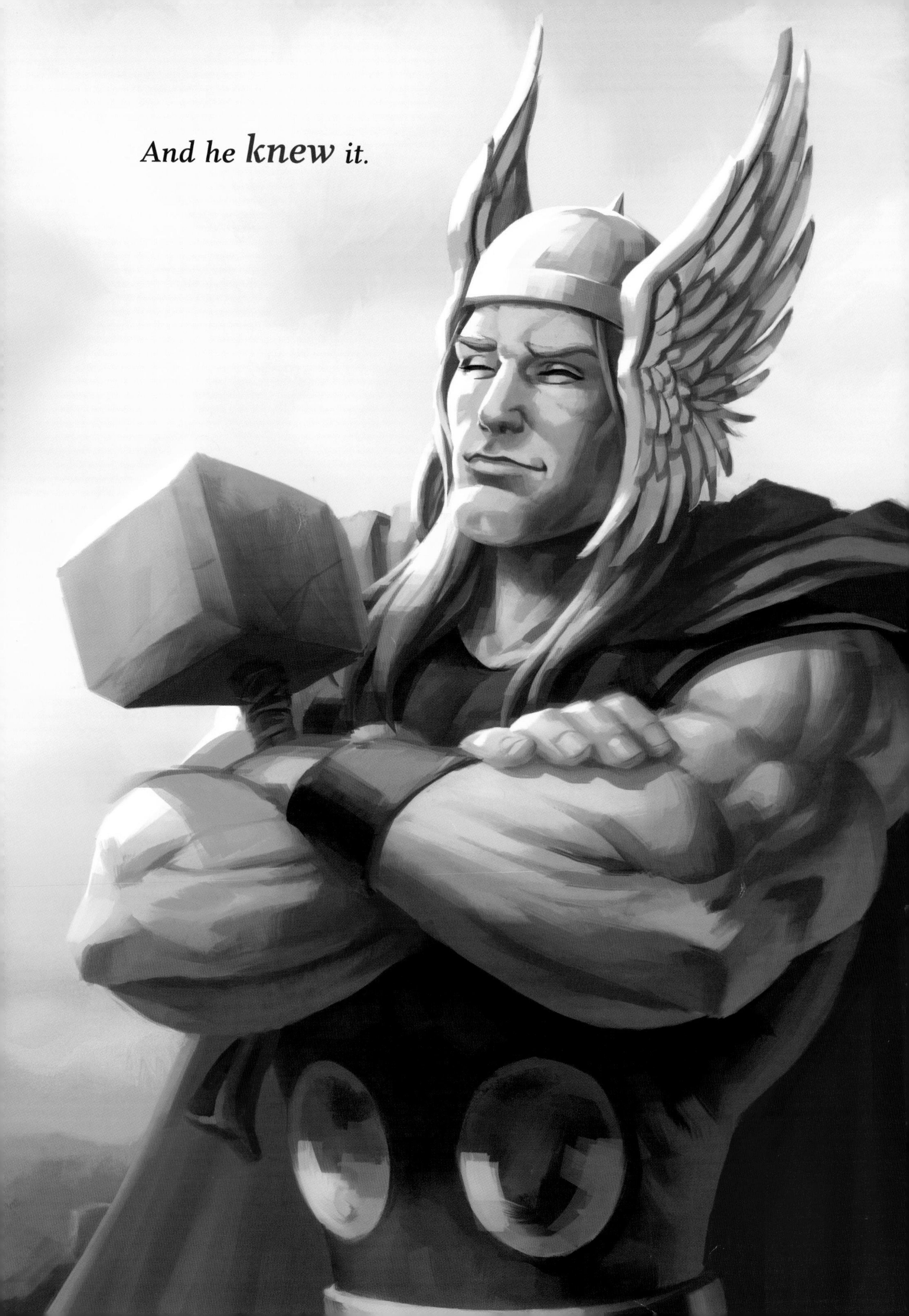

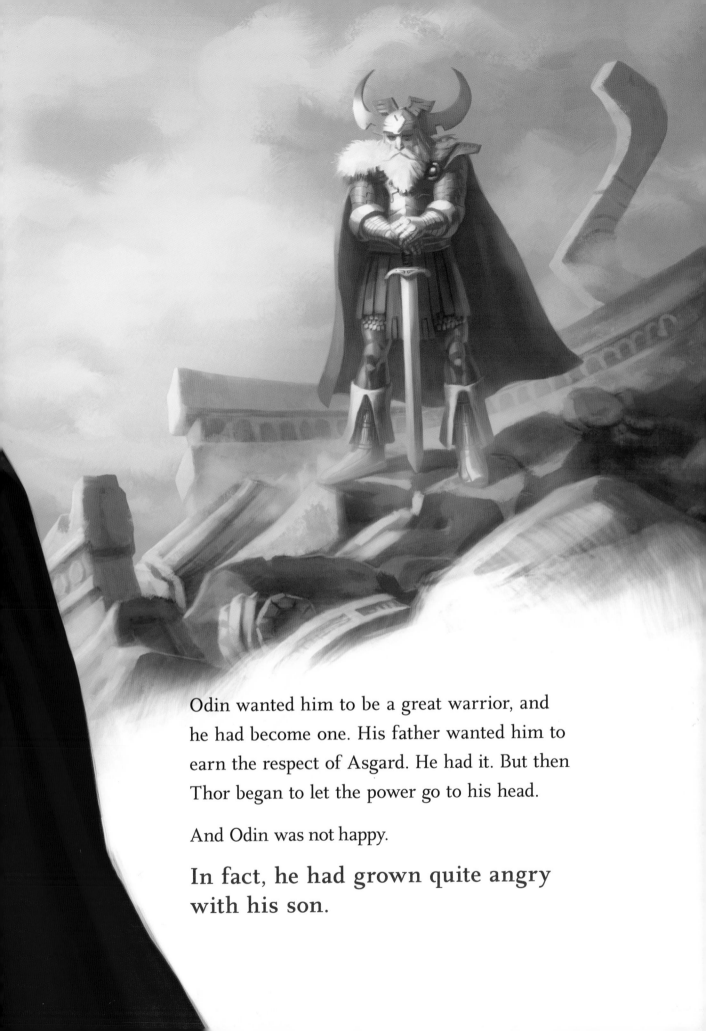

Odin wanted him to be a great warrior, and he had become one. His father wanted him to earn the respect of Asgard. He had it. But then Thor began to let the power go to his head.

And Odin was not happy.

In fact, he had grown quite angry with his son.

Odin called Thor to his throne room. Thor knew that **something was wrong**. His father rarely summoned him in such a harsh tone. Thor was sure that his **jealous brother** Loki had spun some **lie** to get him into trouble.

But nothing could have been further from Thor's mind than what Odin had to say to him.

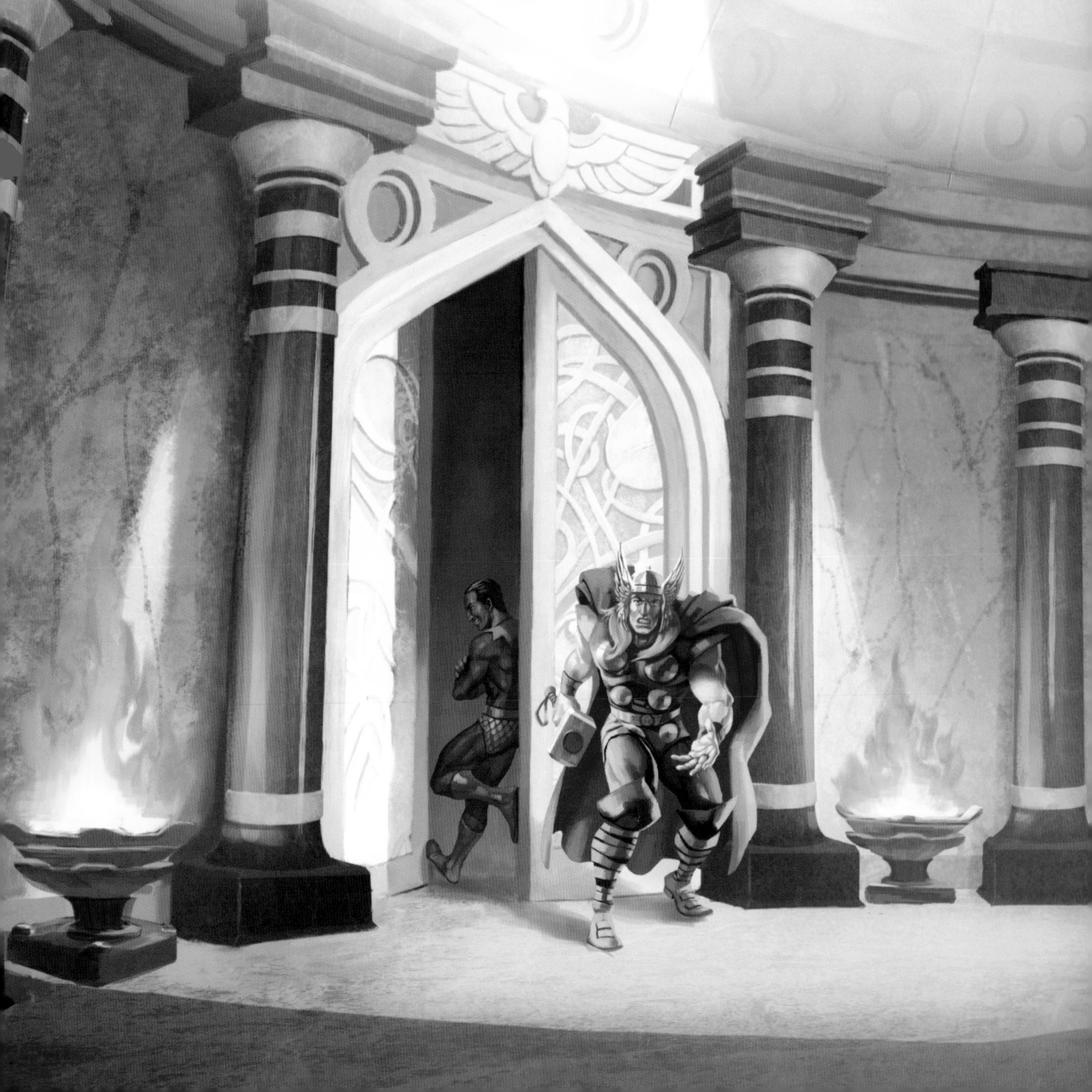

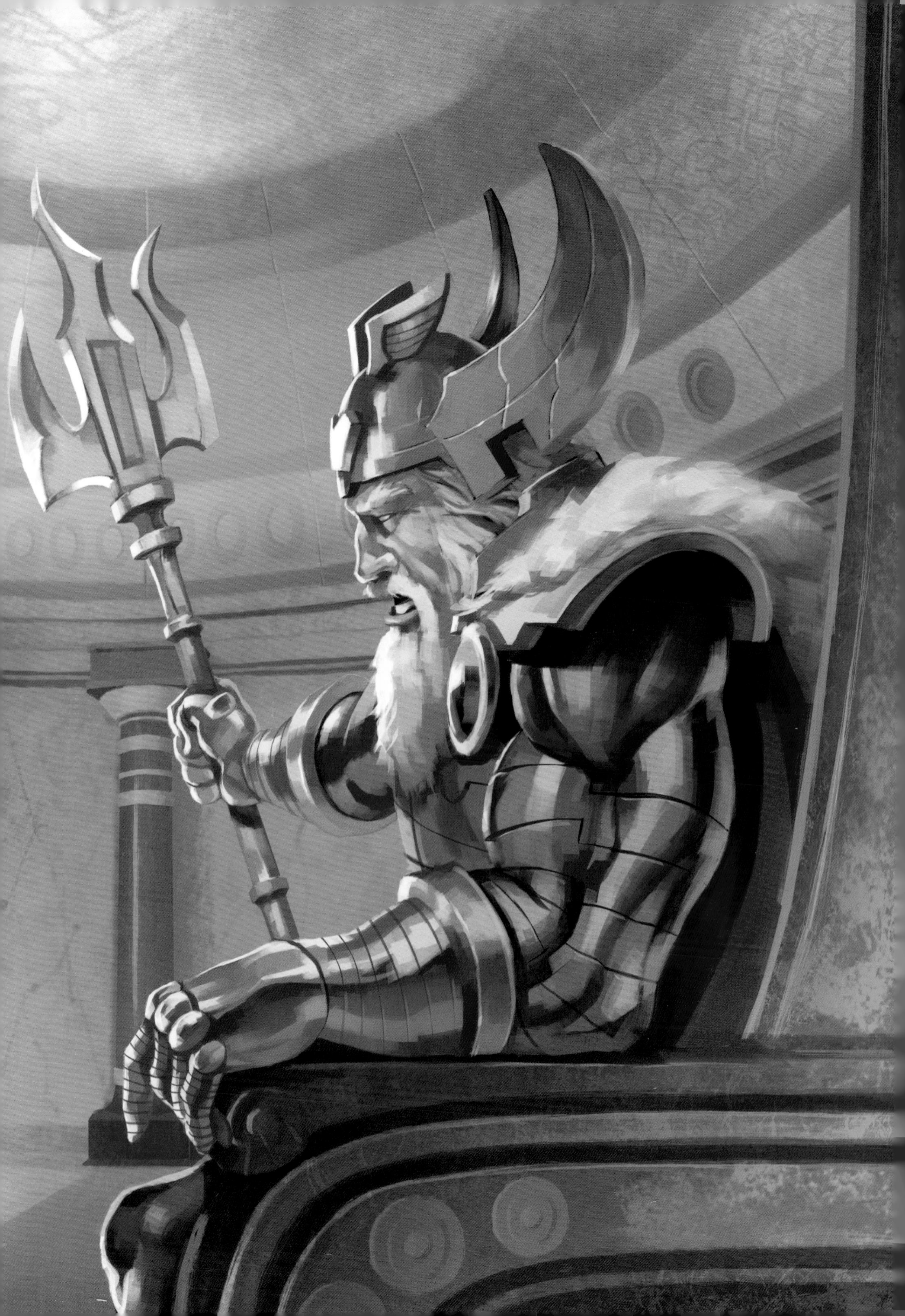

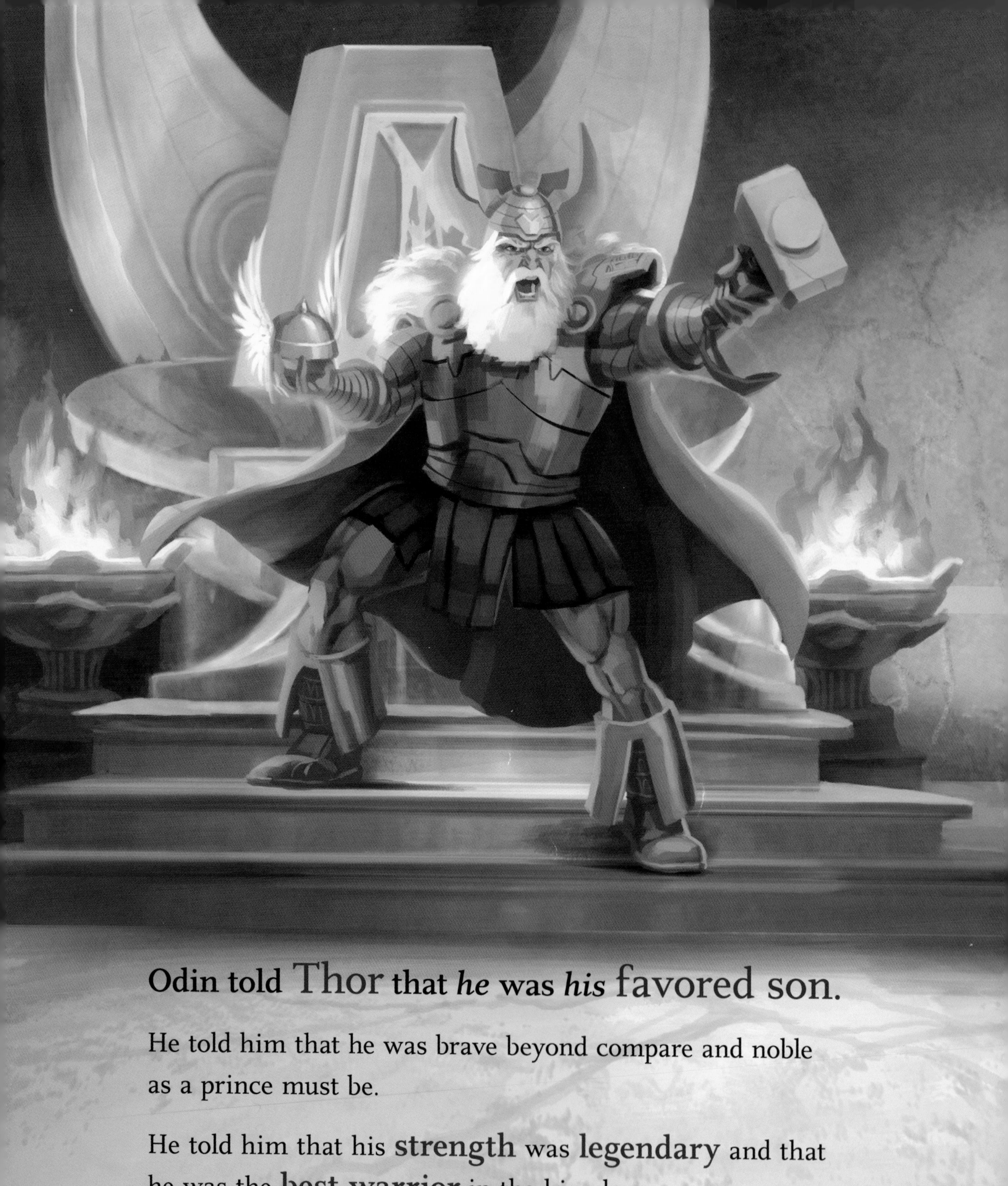

Odin told Thor **that *he* was *his*** favored son.

He told him that he was brave beyond compare and noble as a prince must be.

He told him that his **strength** was **legendary** and that he was the **best warrior** in the kingdom.

But Thor did not know what it meant to be **weak** or to feel **pain**. And without knowing **humility**, Thor could never be a truly **honorable** warrior.

Odin was **angry**. In his rage, he tore Mjolnir from Thor's hand and threw it toward Midgard. Then he stripped Thor of his armor and **sent him to Earth**.

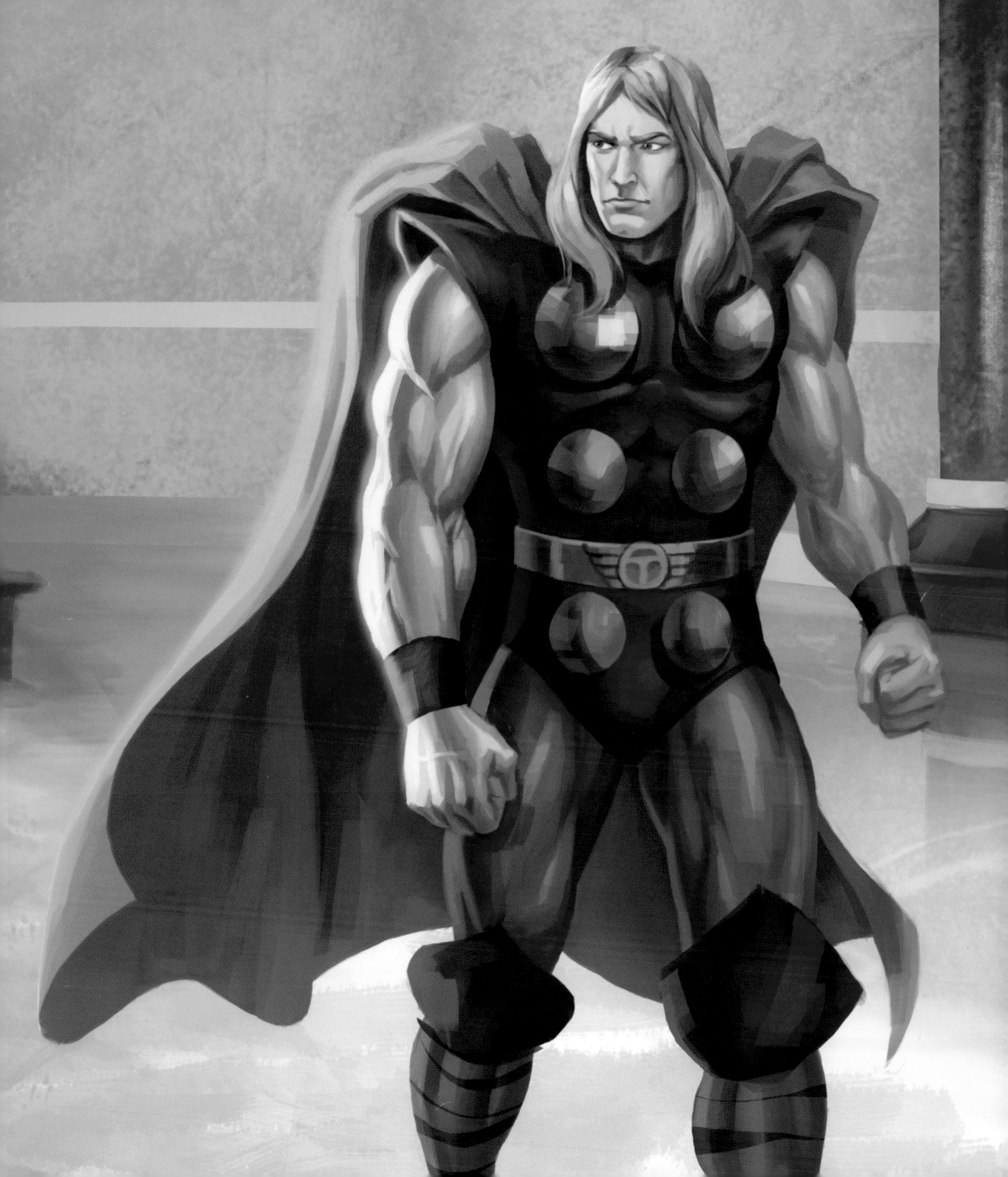

Odin made his son believe that he was a medical student, with an **injured leg**, named **Don Blake**.

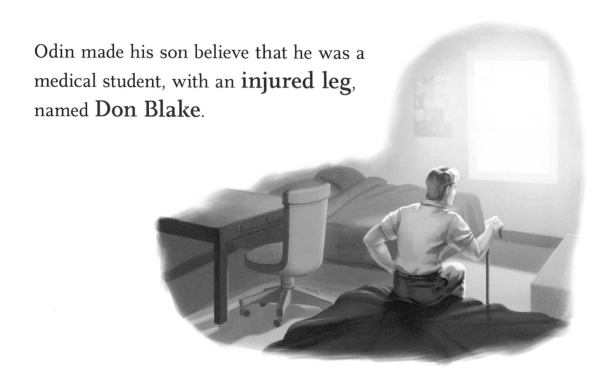

As Blake, Thor learned to **study hard**. At times he thought he might **fail**. But he worked harder than he ever had in Asgard, and in the end he **earned** his degree.

He allowed others to **help** him with his injury. In doing so, he discovered that people were generally **good**. Thor learned to truly love humanity. As a surgeon, he **treated the sick**.

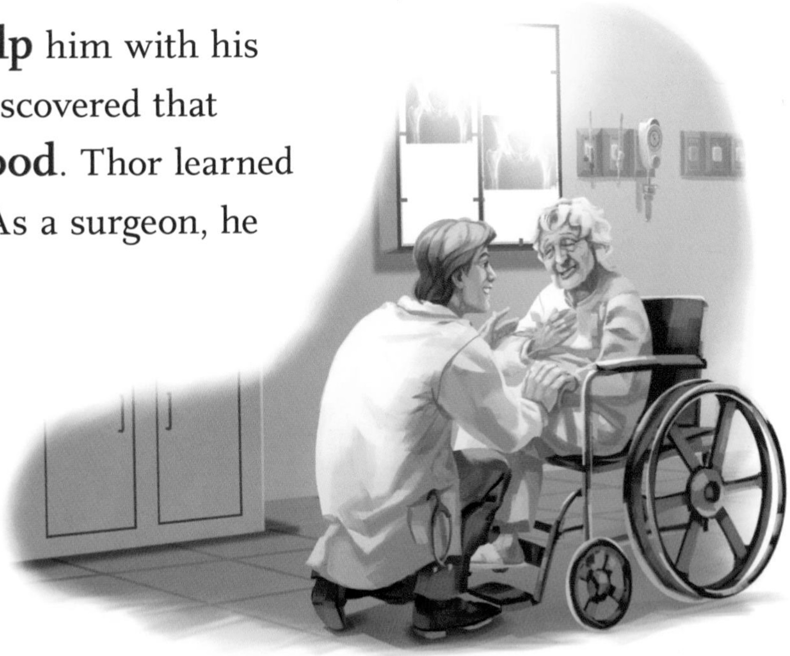

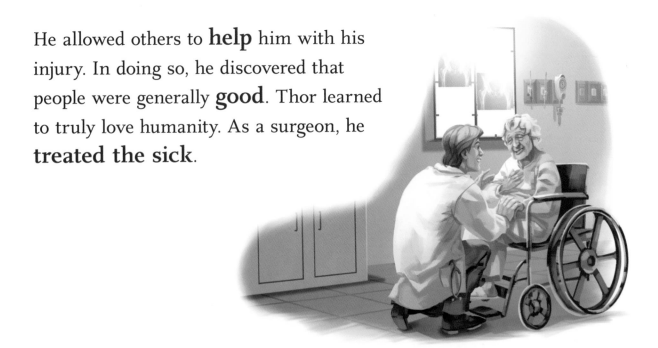

He helped **weak** people find their **strengths**.

And one day, while vacationing in Norway . . .

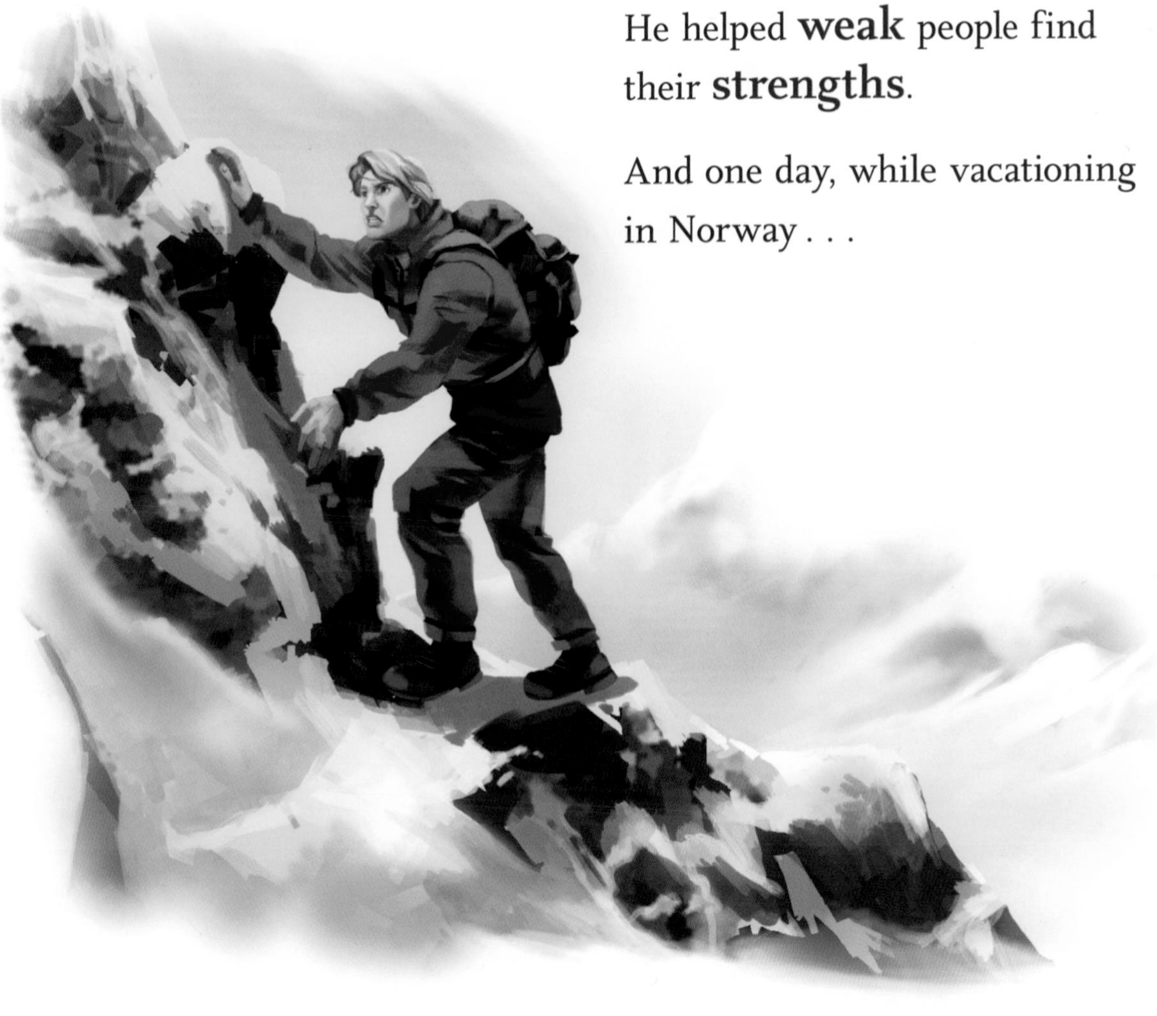

Don Blake found himself **trapped** in a cave.

The only possible exit lay behind a boulder.

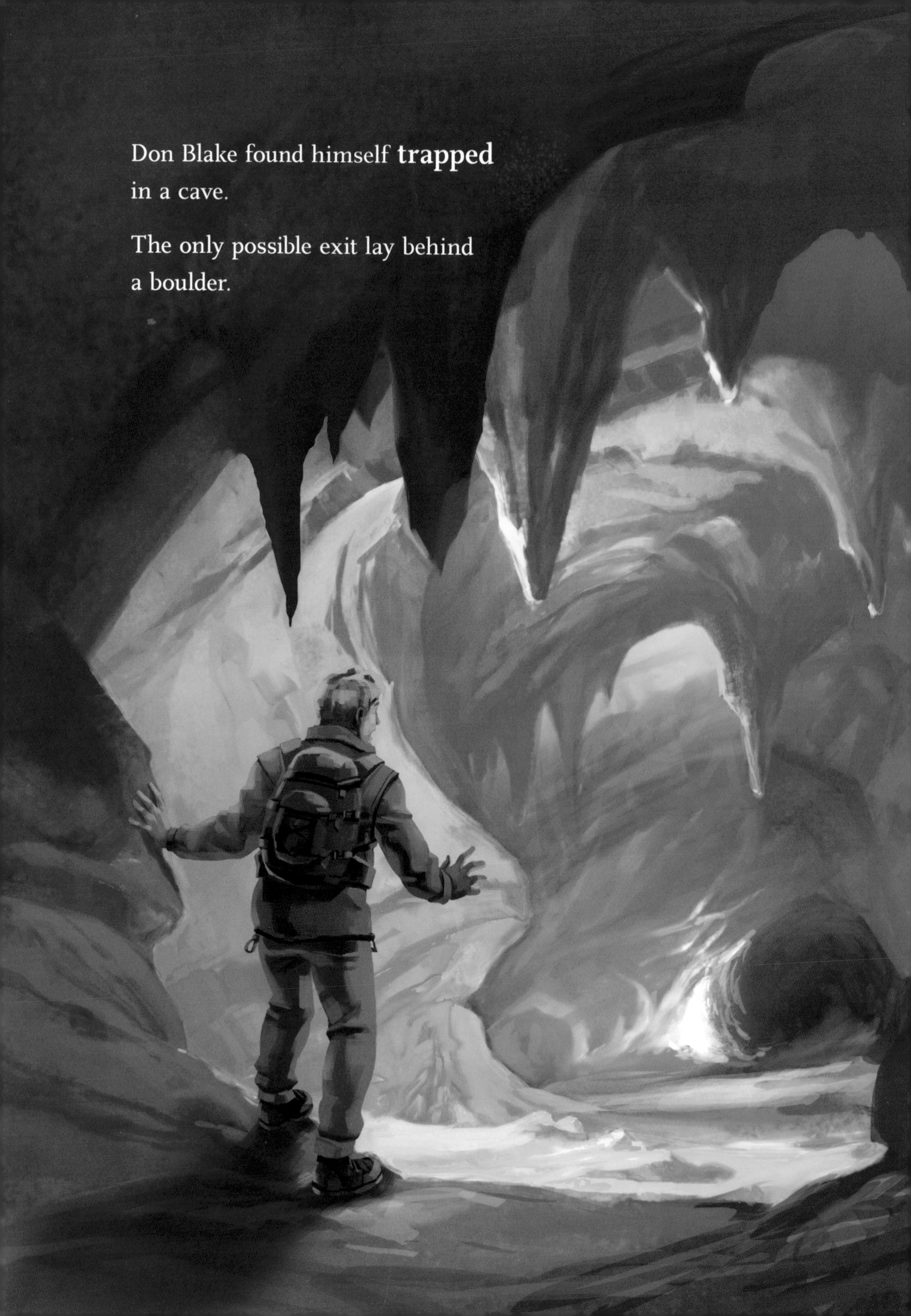

He found a staff on the ground and shoved it under the boulder. He tried with all his might to move the rock.

He pushed and pushed.

Nothing.

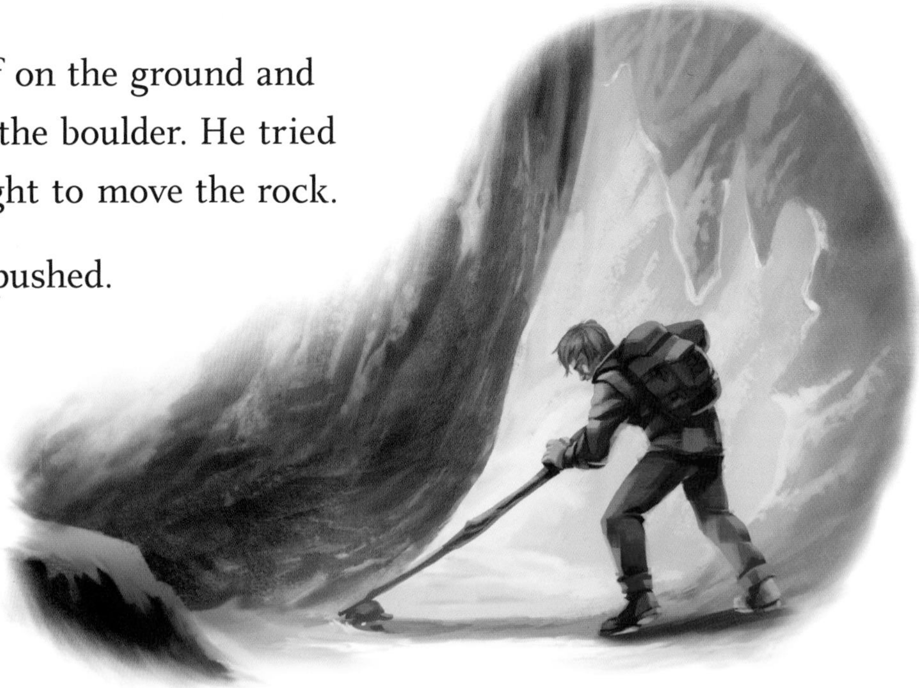

He was so angry that he took the staff and **struck** it on the ground. And that's when it became clear that it was no ordinary stick.

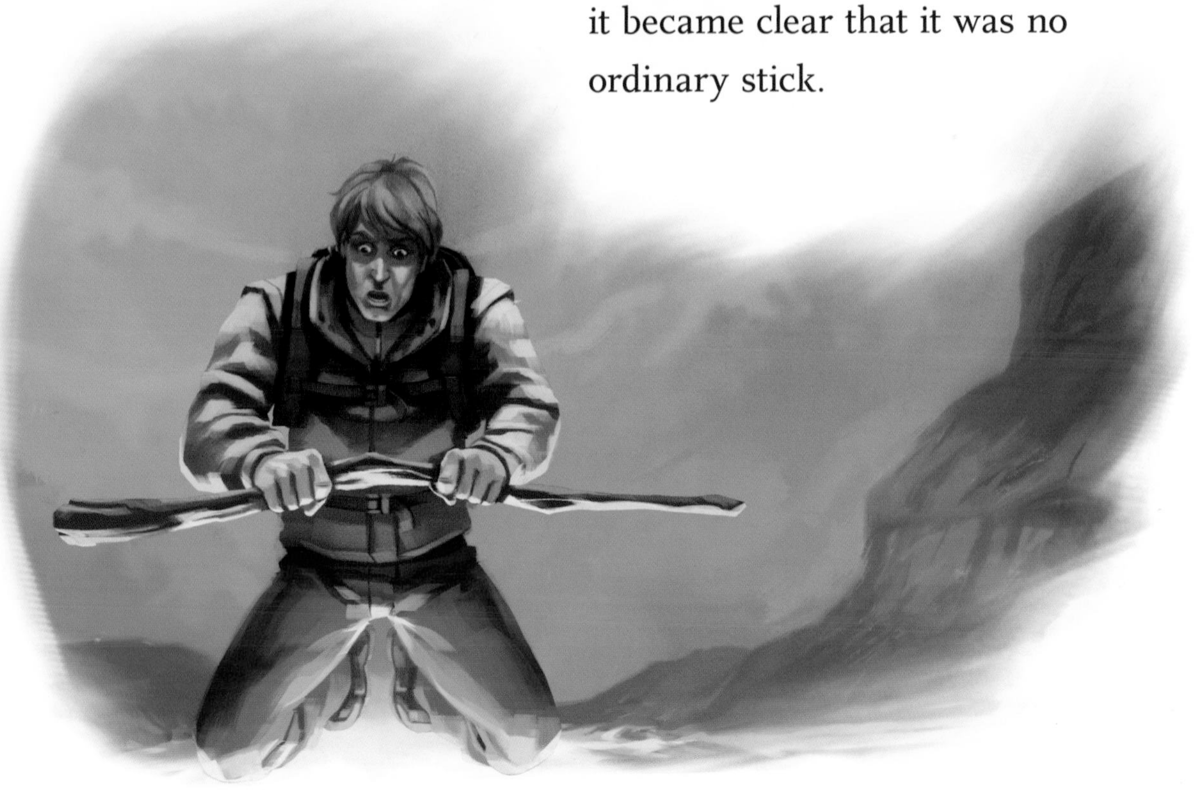

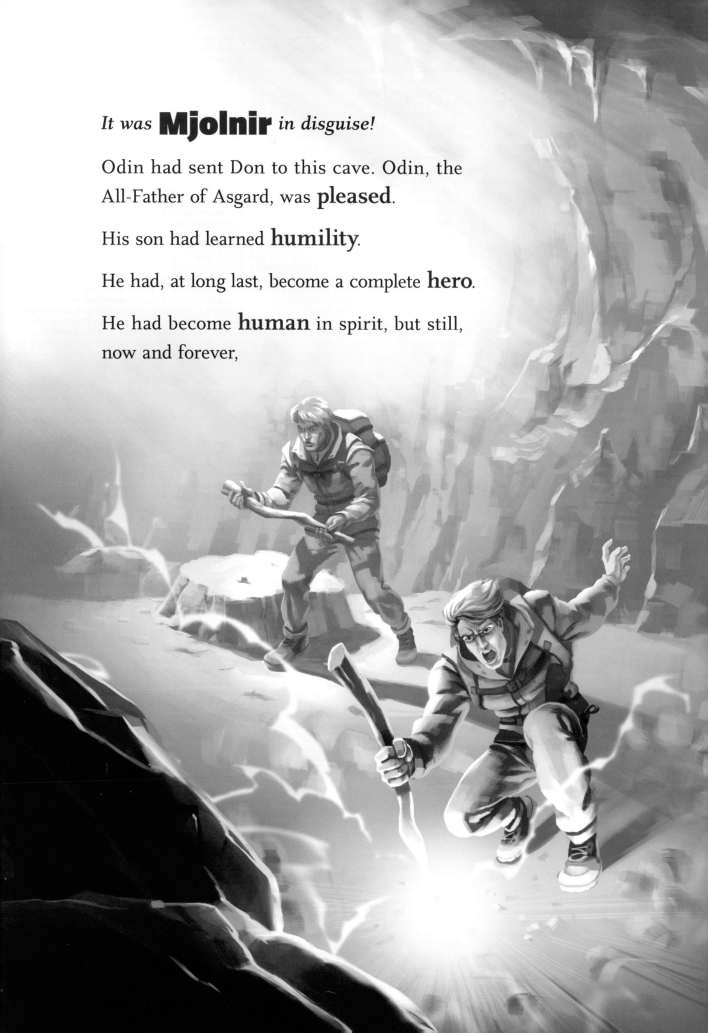

It was **Mjolnir** _in disguise!_

Odin had sent Don to this cave. Odin, the All-Father of Asgard, was **pleased**.

His son had learned **humility**.

He had, at long last, become a complete **hero**.

He had become **human** in spirit, but still, now and forever,

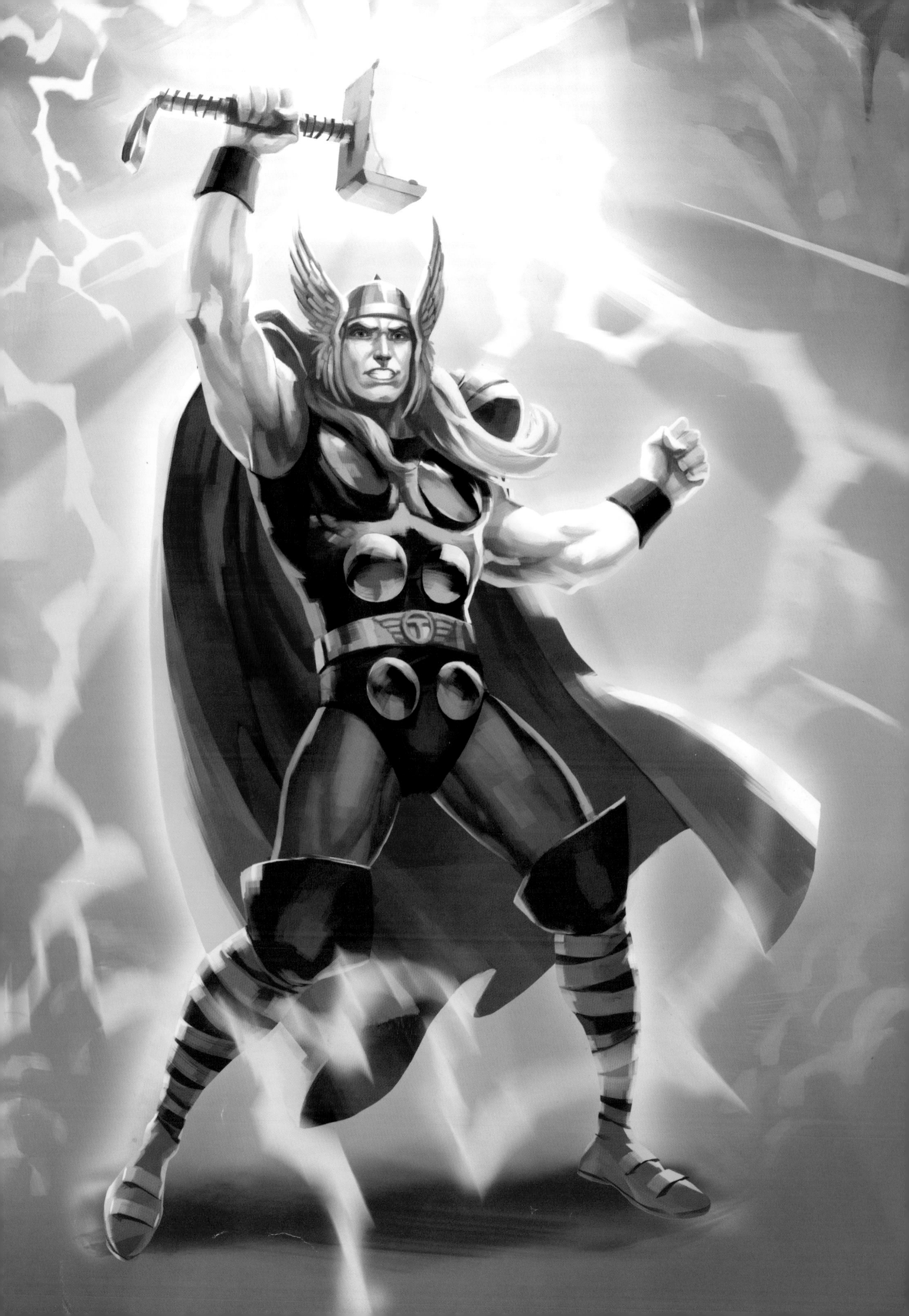

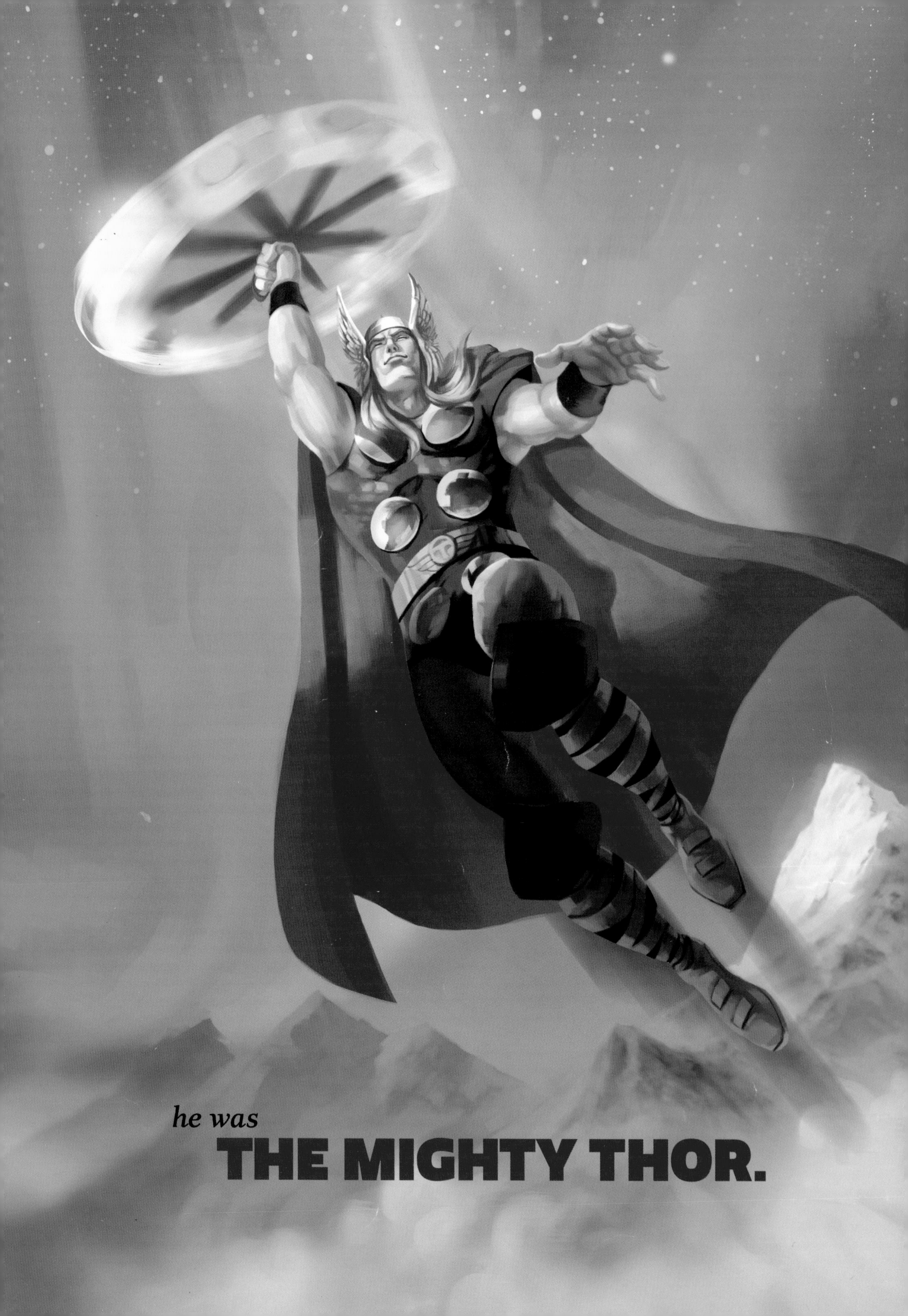

he was
THE MIGHTY THOR.